A Candlelight Ecstasy Romance™

THE MOAN IN HER THROAT WAS STIFLED BY HIS MOUTH UPON HERS . . . .

"Yes," he growled, as she twisted furiously against him, arching herself into his strength with a savage femininity that took her own breath away.

For an instant she faced the thought that this couldn't be her and then she was lost, helplessly swept along on a tide of unfathomable need and desire.

"I will make you mine, little Chandra," he vowed in a harsh rasp. "And then you won't have any more doubts. There will be no more chasing the will-o'-the-wisp you call love. There will be only the reality of you belonging to me!"

CANDLELIGHT ECSTASY ROMANCES™

A MAN'S PROTECTION

Jayne Castle

A CANDLELIGHT ECSTASY ROMANCE™

Published by
Dell Publishing Co., Inc.
1 Dag Hammarskjold Plaza
New York, New York 10017

Dell ® TM 681510, Dell Publishing Co., Inc.

Candlelight Ecstasy Romance™ is a trademark of
Dell Publishing Co., Inc., New York, New York.

ISBN: 0-440-15188-0

Printed in the United States of America

First printing—January 1982

Dear Reader:

In response to your enthusiasm for Candlelight Ecstasy Romances™, we are now increasing the number of titles per month from three to four.

We are pleased to offer you sensuous novels set in America depicting modern American women and men as they confront the provocative problems of a modern relationship.

Throughout the history of the Candlelight line, Dell has tried to maintain a high standard of excellence, to give you the finest in reading pleasure. It is now and will remain our most ardent ambition.

Editor
Candlelight Romances

A MAN'S PROTECTION

CHAPTER ONE

"Good morning!"

Chandra Madison heard the deep sandpaper and velvet tones through the rising clamor of another voice, one that hammered a warning deep in her fogged brain. She knew she ought to pay attention to that inner shout. It spoke with the authority of female instinct and it was screaming at her not to open her eyes; not to acknowledge the reality of the warm, sunny California morning.

But the lazy drawl of the dark, sleep-roughened masculine voice emanating from the pillow next to hers cut through the inner warnings with easy command and confidence.

"The perfect hostess, indeed," Reid Devlin went on, softly teasing. "Harry was absolutely right. Do your services extend to fixing my breakfast?"

Chandra cringed under the sheet, and, calling on more courage than she would have given herself credit for, she forced open her eyes. Overhead the dancing sunlight off the ocean bounced along the ceiling and ricocheted around the chrome and glass room.

It had finally happened, she thought vaguely. She had made it into the southern California fast lane with a vengeance. Only to be run over by the far more experienced traffic already moving in it.

"Hey, honey," the man next to her chuckled huskily, "I'm over here, not on the ceiling!"

A large male hand moved briefly in front of her wide-open hazel eyes, seeking to attract her attention. She wished he wouldn't do that. She wished he would stop talking to her, too. She wished she were a million miles away. Chandra swallowed experimentally and didn't care for the effect on her stomach.

The hand was a strong one, with slightly calloused palms and amazingly sensitive fingertips. Sinewy cords of muscles and veins extended from the wrist along the length of the arm. As if hypnotized, Chandra turned her head slowly to follow the path of tanned skin, with its course sprinkling of copper hairs, first to the elbow and then, as if she couldn't avoid it, all the way to the massive shoulder.

Still scraping together every ounce of her courage, she let the inevitable happen. Her eyes collided with his. And even though the image of him was indelibly printed on her mind she made herself catalog Reid Devlin all over again. It was a kind of penance, she told herself fleetingly.

"How do you feel?" he inquired politely, the glacier gray-blue of his eyes flickering with humor and, perhaps, expectant sympathy.

"As if I'm going to be sick," she managed honestly, her mouth tasting horrible.

"I'm not surprised," he admonished gently, the hard line of his mouth curving into a knowing smile. "Hostesses shouldn't get drunk at their own parties!"

"Your sympathy is, of course, very welcome," she was able to retort grimly, hating him and hating herself even more. Why had she been such a fool? If only Kirby hadn't . . .

Bleakly she forced that line of thought to a crashing halt. She had only herself to blame for this mess. She should have known better than to expect Kirby Latimer was interested in anything other than another superficial California-style relationship. My God! She was twenty-eight years old! Hadn't she learned anything at all about men in this part of the world?

10

And Reid Devlin was no different. True, there was nothing of the handsome, open, living-on-the-surface southern California male look about him. The hawkish nose, the normally inflexible line of his mouth, and the faintly autocratic way he carried his head on the sun-colored column of his neck gave evidence of a life spent in other pursuits than just that of the good life. The broad, smoothly muscled line of his shoulders bespoke his background in the construction industry. Standing, he topped her own five and a half feet by a healthy margin. She guessed he was nearly six feet, two inches.

Yes, he was large and she knew the strength in him all too well. He didn't appear the least bit soft and she knew the hardness in him went deeper than the lean hips and strong thighs.

But he was no different from all the others. The power in him, though vastly more compelling than the superficial charm of other men, was used for the same purposes for which weaker men used their easy manners and casual sophistication. It was used to secure Reid Devlin what he wanted, and last night he had wanted her.

Chandra closed her eyes against the mocking, satisfied expression on his harshly carved features. For some reason the afterglow of the copper streaks in his thick pelt of dark brown hair remained on her eyelids. Or was that some strange effect of the nausea she was experiencing?

"I may not sound overly sympathetic," he told her cheerfully, "but nurses are supposed to be bracing, not sweet and cloying. And I have the distinct impression I'm about to play nurse."

"I'll be all right," she bit out savagely, wondering desperately how she was going to make it to the bathroom in time. "Just give me a few minutes . . ."

"Sorry," he suddenly announced, throwing back the covers and letting his feet hit the rich pile of white on the floor, "but I'd rather clean up the bathroom than this carpet. Come on, hostess, let's go!"

11

He was wearing only a pair of white Jockey shorts, and when Chandra's eyes fluttered momentarily open he was standing beside her, leaning down to scoop her up off the bed.

"No, please!" But her protest was weak, even to her own ears. He ignored it, pulling down the sheet and lifting her into his arms with an effortless ease. Again she closed her eyes, partly to block out the feel of his coppery-haired chest and partly so she wouldn't have to witness her own nudity.

But she wasn't quite nude, she realized abruptly as he carried her across the coldly modern room. She seemed to have on a man's undershirt, which reached to her thighs, and below that she was still wearing her lacy bikini briefs. It wasn't much to be thankful for on this awful morning, but it was something.

"Here you go. I'll hold your head," Reid was saying encouragingly, swinging her gently to her feet in the bathroom. "You'll feel better when you've finished."

God! She didn't want him holding her while she was sick! Things were mortifying enough.

"Please, leave me alone," she begged. "I'll be all right."

But already she was leaning over the white porcelain bowl and once started she couldn't seem to exert any control over her nauseated body. Reid never left her side and part of her acknowledged his care.

"Feel better?" he asked kindly when it was all over.

Chandra got her eyes opened again and nodded weakly. "Yes. Thank you." What else could one say under the circumstances?

"You look like hell," he noted critically.

"Sorry," she tried to snarl scathingly. But the word barely made it past her throat as she caught sight of her forlorn figure in the mirrored bathroom wall. He was right.

Her long tawny hair was no longer in the neat, habitual knot. It cascaded around her shoulders rather limply. The hazel eyes with their long lashes, which normally went well with the lionskin-colored hair, seemed devoid of the lively intelligence that normally resided there. Oh, the intelligence was still around, she thought irritably, it just didn't look too lively.

The mouth that usually curved so readily and added energy and animation to what Chandra privately felt was an ordinary set of features looked bruised and sulky in the bathroom light. Normally the faint upward slant of the eyes made the high cheekbones appear a little more dramatic than they really were and the laughing mouth drew attention away from the less than classical jawline. Normally it was a face full of personality. Normally.

Without any interest, except a morbid curiosity, Chandra let her eyes examine the slender length of her figure in the mirror. Small, rounded breasts thrust against the white cotton undershirt, tapering down to a curving, narrow waist. Her hips were full, more so than she would have liked, but the length of leg was reasonably good. She did a lot of swimming. On her least self-critical days she might have wished for a touch more height and a little more of the sexy, inviting California look and let it go at that. This morning the self-criticism didn't know where to stop.

"Next step is a shower," Reid was declaring conversationally.

"I'll manage on my own," she told him urgently as his hands grasped the edge of the undershirt and started to haul it over her head. Fretfully she slapped at his fingers. "Leave me alone, Reid!"

"What are you getting so excited about?" he demanded with a knowing smile as he ignored her efforts. "You just spent the night in my bed!"

The words defeated her. She didn't have the strength or the will to fight him this morning. And he was right. Horribly, humiliatingly right. She had spent the night in his bed.

"That's better," he approved as she turned away from the mirror and stood dejectedly as he stripped her few garments from her body.

"In you get," he prodded, adjusting the nozzle of the invigorating hot spray of water in the huge, tiled shower.

Out of some residual sense of modesty she kept her back to him, stepping under the shower and letting it drench her. How was it possible to feel so ill and not be genuinely sick? She had never been drunk before in her life. She knew how to handle liquor. But last night the margaritas from Reid's blender seemed never-ending, and every time she had looked at Kirby Latimer and his wife she had reached for another. His wife!

"Here's some shampoo," Reid said behind her, and with a start Chandra realized he was standing in the shower with her. She didn't dare glance around. He would be completely naked now. "Stand still and I'll wash your hair for you."

Teeth clenched, her hand braced against the white tiled wall, she tried to keep her balance while he speared his fingers through her wet hair. The lather grew increasingly thicker as he worked and she wondered how he could be so full of energy this morning. It wasn't fair.

Nor did it seem fair that she should have to reenter the real world, either, she told herself sadly as the hot water began to do its work. Slowly, under the impact of Reid's ministrations and the stinging spray, the mind-numbing fog began to dissipate. It was not a blessing.

For one thing she was becoming aware that now her hair had been rinsed, Reid was turning his attention to other parts of her body. Soap in hand, he was starting to scrub her back. Nervously she tried to step out of reach.

"Where do you think you're going?" he murmured deeply, his arm circling her waist to pull her back against him. The ensuing shock to her nervous system went a long way toward clearing out more of the cobwebs.

"I can bathe myself," she told him stonily, hating the

14

fine trembling in her limbs. She was violently aware of the slippery, binding pressure of his arm and the nearness of his body as he bent his head to drop a small kiss on her temple.

"Relax. Hostess duties are over," he assured her throatily. "I'm no longer paying you to supervise my party and entertain my guests. At least, I *hope* I'm not still paying you. At your rates, I'll be bankrupt before you recover from your hangover!"

She flushed vividly and knew the red color was seeping up into her cheeks from the tops of her breasts.

"Reid, I feel enough of a fool as it is. Please don't tease me this morning!"

"A fool, hmm? Not nearly as big a fool as I felt last night when I cornered good old Harry and told him I wanted his mistress!"

"Reid! You didn't!" Chandra closed her eyes once again. On any other morning she might have found the news hilarious. The thought of Reid Devlin having made an idiot of himself like that would have brightened her entire week. But nothing could brighten this morning.

"Damn right I did, and it's all your fault for letting me think he had a claim on you, Chandra Madison," Reid told her feelingly. "If you weren't so hung over I'd be tempted to beat you for what you put me through during the past week and a half!"

"You're the one who leaped to the conclusion I was Harry's lover!" she reminded him gamely, struggling to revive some of her natural spirit.

"I had a lot of encouragement from you and don't you dare pretend otherwise," he shot back ruefully, his free hand playing with the wet tendrils of her hair. "Every time I tried to get your attention on something besides the party I'd hired you to plan, you threw Harry into my face!"

"It seemed simpler that way," she sighed morosely, aware that in the end it hadn't mattered. She had still wound up in Reid Devlin's arms last night. Nothing could change that awful fact.

"A simple method of keeping me at bay? I've got news for you, sweetheart, nothing would have worked for long. Don't you know how intriguing you are, little Chandra? All that bright, breezy, go-to-hell nonchalance on the outside and all that vibrant warmth on the inside. Didn't you know that every minute you spent with me you were practically daring me to call your bluff?"

"No!" she squeaked, alarmed and knowing it was far too late to be alarmed. The damage was done. "That's not true! If I'd known for a second that you were one of those men who wants a woman just because she belongs to another man, I'd have tried something else!"

His arm around her stiffened warningly, and she was painfully aware of the heat and strength in his thighs. She couldn't help but be aware of it because of the fierce way he was holding her against him.

"You are indeed the bigger fool if you thought I only went after you because I believed you were Harry's mistress." He gave her a small shake and she sensed the mild annoyance in him. "I happen to value my friendship with Harry Templeton. Do you know how I felt last night when I decided I couldn't stand it any longer and dragged him out onto the balcony to tell him I intended to take you away from him?"

"I trust he laughed in your face!"

"Oh, he did. In fact, I didn't think he was going to be able to stop laughing," Reid admitted dryly. "At first I thought it was because he assumed I didn't have a chance in hell of convincing you to leave him. Then, when he'd finally calmed down and told me you were free as a bird . . ."

Chandra felt the shame flooding her veins. Free as a bird. Until last night she hadn't really traveled in that section of the fast lane. Until last night she had sought relationships based on an abiding love and understanding.

16

There had been heartaches and disappointments enough in the past, but at least she'd gone after her dreams with an earnest heart. A heart that had wanted to give and receive love. Never had she been reduced to the level of a woman who got drunk and threw herself into bed with the nearest available male! Perhaps the local life-style had caught up with her. Perhaps she was learning to live with the reality of the kind of relationships so abundant here. Instinctively her mind denied it.

"Free as a bird," she repeated aloud, hating the pathetic thread in her own words. She had to get a grip on herself. Last night had been a disaster, but she was old enough to pull herself back together after disasters. Look how she'd managed to survive that devastation four years ago. Yes, she was old enough and strong enough, she assured herself bravely.

"When I finally realized what he was trying to tell me, I didn't know whether to find you in the crowd and kiss you breathless or beat you senseless. Harry thinks it's all terribly amusing, you know."

"Harry has a weird sense of humor."

"He told me the two of you had never been lovers and that he would be delighted to see you and I have a relationship . . ."

"Relationship. What a delightfully modern and useful word." Chandra didn't even attempt to keep the scorn out of her voice. She could almost feel Reid's dark brow climbing in cool amusement.

"Isn't it, though?" he volunteered easily, and she thought for the first time since she had awakened that some of the icy flavor of his voice was back. It was with a start that she realized it had been missing so far that morning. She had grown so accustomed to it during the preceding week that things seemed more normal when he utilized it.

"It does cover a multitude of situations," she went on determinedly. "How else could one describe last night

17

without resorting to such phrases as 'one night stand'?" She was only hurting herself, she knew, but she thought she deserved it.

"Well," he retorted obligingly, " 'one night stand' does imply something more than merely sharing the same bed." There was a testing, baiting quality in his voice.

"It implies a night of cheap, easy sex!" she declared wretchedly, thankful for the rush of water over her skin. At least it provided some stimulus.

"Exactly," he countered obliquely. "Which is why 're-lationship' is probably a better euphemism for our situation. Everybody naturally assumes there's sex involved, but . . ."

"Reid, what the devil are you talking about?" Chandra demanded, too exhausted to figure out his rambling words.

"Sex," he reminded her simply.

"I know, but . . ."

"Or lack thereof," he concluded smoothly.

Chandra froze beneath the heat of the water. She was still clamped tightly against him and she could have sworn a tremor of laughter had coursed through his lean frame.

"Lack thereof?" she hazarded cautiously. "Reid, are you telling me . . . Are you saying that we didn't . . . I didn't . . . ?"

She tore herself free of his grip to swing precariously around and face him. And immediately turned back to face the opposite wall, unable to confront the amusement in the gray-blue eyes or the uncompromising male length of him. He towered over her and she was unbearably aware of him from her head to her toes.

"What's the matter, honey?" he asked with a patently false concern, his hands descending to her shoulders to massage the muscles there. "Can't you remember?"

"Tell me!" she begged, slapping the tiled wall with the flat of her hand in sheer frustration.

18

"Unfortunately, there's not much to tell," he informed her wryly. "What's the last thing you recall?"

She drew a deep, shaky breath, trying desperately to sort out the kaleidoscopic images of the previous night. "I remember . . ." She stopped and gulped another breath. "I remember you carrying me into the bedroom and . . ." Grimly she made herself continue. "And being on the bed. You . . . you undressed me, I think . . ."

"Umm," he agreed unhelpfully. "I am good for a couple of things like undressing you and helping you with your hangover."

"I remember you climbing into bed beside me," she mumbled hopelessly. The image was shockingly clear. She had been luxuriating in the feel of the cool sheets, marveling at the numbing effect of the alcohol and thinking vaguely that Kirby Latimer wasn't worth her tears; not when she had a man like this to cling to. Reid was large and strong and he seemed to envelop her in his power. She had put out a hand to touch the thick mat of curling hair on his chest; remembered him smiling down at her with male promise and anticipation as he lowered his head to take her lips . . ..

"Climbing into bed beside you was about as far as things got, I'm afraid," Reid told her calmly, his hands still kneading her neck and shoulders. "You, my charming little hostess, passed out on me. A great blow to my ego, I can promise you! Although the humor of the situation did not escape me," he went on laconically, laughter in his words again. "That doesn't mean I don't intend to collect full payment for your mistreatment of me, however. First you nearly drive me crazy letting me think you were Harry's and then, when I finally get you into my bed, you calmly go off to sleep without showing any appreciation at all for my marvelous technique!"

"Oh, Reid, is that the truth?" she begged, feeling some of the self-disgust lighten. It certainly wasn't through any

19

fault of hers that she had not gone the whole route but it was something to cling to in the midst of the crisis.

"I'm afraid so," he sighed regretfully. "And somehow," he joked, "I just couldn't bring myself to carry on without you! Silly of me, I know, but my pride demands that you be fully alert and aware of what we're sharing when the time comes!"

"Thank you, Reid," Chandra muttered truthfully, renewed energy starting to flow into her body. She pulled aside the shower curtain, averting her eyes from his blatant masculinity, and grabbed for a white towel. Everything in Reid's house seemed white or glass or chrome. Somebody had told her his ex-wife had decorated it shortly before leaving him to "find herself."

She wrenched the nearest towel off the rack and hastily wrapped it around her dripping figure, aware that he was watching her from the shower stall.

"You seem to be recovering rather rapidly," he observed quietly.

She could feel his eyes trying to compel hers and refused to give in to the pressure.

"It's not much after the way I behaved, but I do feel some measure of relief," she admitted, reaching for another towel with which to dry her hair.

She heard him turn off the water and push back the white shower curtain. Dimly, her hair in her face, she groped for the doorknob. She had to get out of there. He seemed to be dominating the entire bathroom, large as it was. A part of her could still feel his hands in her hair.

She was almost out the door and back into the bedroom when she felt his arm close almost casually around her waist and turn her around to confront him.

"What now?" she demanded with the beginnings of irritation mixing into her words. She could feel her normal self-confidence starting to return and the sensation was devastatingly wonderful.

"You've got both towels," he explained coolly, reaching for the one around her hair. "Mind loaning me one?"

"Of . . . of course," she agreed hurriedly, not finding his nudity any easier to handle here in the bedroom than it had been in the bath. Her body kept remembering snatches of scenes from the night. There was a memory of warmth into which she had curled and the recollection of a pleasantly heavy arm lying possessively across her breasts. Quickly she turned away and began hunting for her clothes.

"I hung them in the closet," he told her quietly, rubbing himself dry idly while he watched her frantic search.

"Thank you," she said again, instinct telling her she was going to feel much more in command of the situation once she was dressed. What a ghastly situation! But not, thank heaven, quite as bad as it might have been . . . .

She found the green sheath hanging neatly beside a row of shirts in the closet, and beneath it, on the floor, were her sandals. She flung the dress over her head, heedless of the damp tendrils of hair, and then remembered her briefs were in the bathroom. There was no bra to worry about. She hadn't worn one with the halter-necked dress. In spite of the fact that very few of her acquaintances bothered wearing bras she still wondered grimly what Reid had thought when he'd undressed her. But how much worse could he think of her? She had already proven herself the most casual of dates!

No, damnit! She hadn't been a date. She had been a hired hostess for his fancy friends from San Francisco. Who would have guessed Kirby Latimer, her fast-living, fun-loving journalist, would have been among the guests? Or that he was married?

The grim thought pounded at her brain as she whirled shakily to head back toward the bathroom. Reid was standing beside a dressing table, stepping into a pair of jeans. He clasped the wide-buckled belt around his lean

21

waist as she groped on the floor of the bathroom for her underwear.

"Does all this scurrying about mean you're going to rush into the kitchen and fix my breakfast?" he asked quizzically as she straightened in front of the mirror and began running her fingers through her damp hair in an effort to comb it.

"What do you think?" she shot back frostily, wanting only to escape. "I'm going to head for home as soon as I can. I have managed to totally humiliate myself and all I want to do right now is hide!" Her hazel eyes flashed gold sparks as she met his sardonic gaze in the mirror. Just looking at him made her uncomfortable now. He had very nearly gotten what he wanted last night and he knew it. She had seen the satisfaction in his eyes this morning.

But why should he have appeared so satisfied if they hadn't actually made love? Nervously, Chandra licked her lower lip. He had told her the truth, hadn't he? Oh, dear God! Hadn't he?

"What's the matter, honey?" he asked softly. He had finished buttoning an open-necked yellow shirt and was absently rolling up the sleeves. His hair gleamed wetly from the shower and she could see the touches of gray at the temples, revealed in the morning sunlight. She had guessed him to be somewhere in his late thirties, probably thirty-seven or thirty-eight. He looked every inch the super-casual, self-confident, successful southern California businessman that he was. He might have started out in construction but he owned the company today.

"Are you really that embarrassed just because you had a couple of margaritas too many and passed out on me?" His deep voice ruffled her nerve endings in a way that sent shivers down her spine.

With great effort Chandra stifled a desire to scream at him. After all, she would never have to see this man again after today, even if he was a friend of Harry's!

"Yes, damnit! I am embarrassed!" She whirled to face

him, eyes blazing. "I *am* Chandra's Organized, Inc., re-member? My firm had the job of handling that party last night and the firm's chief representative, its president, got drunk and acted like an idiot! She woke up to find herself in bed with a man she barely knows and doesn't particu-larly like. One who is everything she actively dislikes in a man. All southern California machismo and money! Fur-thermore, that man has made it abundantly clear he's a believer in short-term relationships and that his interest in me is temporary at best. . . ." She gulped air.

"Chandra!" he began determinedly, stepping forward. She flung out a hand to stop him.

"Stay away from me! Whatever impression I may have given you last night, it's false. The truth is, I don't want you or any other man like you touching me!"

"Chandra, shut up!" he snapped, the anger beginning to swirl like a shark in the icy depths of his eyes. "What are you so upset about? If you didn't want to get drunk and wind up in my bed then why in hell did you do it?"

"Good question!" she taunted furiously, wishing the pounding in her head would go away. But perhaps that was better than the nausea earlier. If only she didn't feel so much like crying. She had to get away to where she could lick her wounds in silence!

"Then answer it," he shot back meaningfully, his hands planted squarely on his hips as he glared down at her slender figure. "Was it because of Harry Templeton, after all? Are you in love with the man? Are you angry that he gave you up without a fight?"

"Don't be ridiculous!" she grated. "Harry told you the truth. Not that it makes any difference! I'm not a com-modity to be handed off from one man to another!"

"I didn't mean it like that, honey," he began placating-ly, clearly realizing he'd phrased it badly.

"Yes you did!" she stormed, wondering if her head was going to split. "You think of women as passing playthings and don't bother denying it. Harry told me!"

23

"He did?" Reid looked struck by the news.

"He told me all about how your wife left you a year ago and how you've sworn never to marry again. I know all about your opinion of marriage as an archaic institution ill-suited to the California life-style. And you, yourself, have implied a certain thirst for casual affairs!" she accused.

"What I've been implying during the past few days is a certain thirst for you, you little spitfire. And when I finally land you in bed, what happens? You go out like a light, leaving me very, very thirsty!"

She flashed him a sudden, searching look. "You were telling me the truth, then?"

"That we didn't make love?" The glacial eyes narrowed. "What's it to you?"

"Reid!" The wide hazel eyes pleaded with him.

Instantly he seemed to relent. "All right, all right. No, we didn't make love."

Her lashes lowered in relief. Gathering her strength, she headed toward the door. "Then there's nothing left to say. I'll be on my way. You wouldn't happen to know where my purse wound up, would you?"

"Relax, Chandra," he bit out with a small hint of savagery. "You're not going anywhere."

"Is that so?" she challenged, turning at bay.

"Damn right. You're in no condition to drive. That Porsche of yours already has enough dents in it!"

"That's hardly any business of yours!" she snapped, goaded. Criticism of her driving was a definite sore point with her and she didn't need any vulnerable areas attacked this morning!

"Chandra, climb down off your armored tank and be reasonable. You feel lousy. Your head is probably about to kill you and your stomach is undoubtedly still wobbly." There was a soothing element in his words, as if he were trying to stroke back the ruffled feathers.

And that, thought Chandra sadly, was probably all he

24

saw in the situation. A small case of ruffled feathers. She just wished he hadn't been so accurate about her physical condition.

"Now, why don't you relax and come on into the kitchen? I'll make you a nice cup of coffee and some poached eggs. You'll feel a lot better when you've got some decent food in you. I've also got a good supply of aspirin tablets."

He came toward her and she realized he was about to take hold of her arm. Hastily she tugged at the door, intent on escape. But, either because of her weakened condition or simply because he was so much stronger and faster than she was, he caught her.

"It occurs to me," he went on with bland purposefulness, guiding her down the skylit hall, "that there are a few unanswered questions about last night. Questions that, in my eagerness to get you into bed, for all the good it did me, I overlooked."

She slanted a hateful glance up at him. "What are you talking about?"

"The issue you, yourself, raised, sweetheart. Why did you get drunk on the job and let me carry you off to bed?"

CHAPTER TWO

The caterers Chandra had hired for the evening had cleaned before leaving, and the glass and chrome house appeared its normal, thoroughly neat, thoroughly cold self in the balmy morning light.

"Here," Reid ordered brusquely, pushing her gently onto a white leather kitchen stool in front of a glass-topped counter. "Sit still and hold your head while I find the aspirin and put on the coffee."

She might resent taking the orders from him, Chandra thought gloomily, cradling her head and staring blindly out to sea, but when the instructions made perfect sense to her ravaged body it was hard to put up a fight.

She heard him moving efficiently around the huge designer kitchen with its stylish butcher block center island and the spectacular view of the La Jolla surf.

California real estate and the construction industry had been good to Reid Devlin, she reflected, not for the first time. The sleek cedar and glass house perched high on a cliff overlooking the ocean went well with the rest of its expensive neighbors in this charming, well-to-do community just outside of San Diego. La Jolla was full of elegant boutiques and arts and crafts shops, and was charmingly picturesque. The Spanish-flavored San Diego area encompassed several lovely seaside villages but this one was definitely among the most exotic. Reid seemed to fit in perfectly with the affluent life-style.

"First things first," he was saying firmly, plunking two

white tablets down on the counter alongside a glass of water. "Here's the aspirin. Coffee will be ready in a minute."

"Reid, I'm not sure I can keep anything down," she began with painful honesty.

"Try," he said gruffly, and turned away to drag out a pot. A copper-bottomed pot, she noticed. Everything first class. She wondered if his ex-wife had designed the kitchen herself or had a professional do it. Deliberately she put the thought out of her head and swallowed the tablets.

There was a moment of blissful silence as the coffee was prepared and set before her in a steaming mug. Chandra eyed it warily.

"The next drug on the list?" she asked dryly.

"We'll try them all," he told her with a quirking tilt of his hard mouth. "Aspirin, caffeine, and protein. Something's bound to work. You're looking better already."

"Impossible."

"Well, at least your spirit's been returning to normal ever since you got out of the shower," he pursued with earnest cheerfulness as he removed eggs from the refrigerator.

"You mean ever since I discovered I had the sense to pass out at the appropriate moment last night!" she couldn't resist correcting. She wasn't going to have him thinking she was reviving simply because of his care!

His eyes met hers as he shut the refrigerator door, cool assessment in the gray-blue ice. "Would it have been so bad if we'd made love last night?"

She went first hot and then cold under his unrelenting scrutiny.

"Yes! For heaven's sake, Reid, we hardly know each other! You're merely a client that Harry recommended." She looked away from him, concentrating on the bright sunlight on the ocean below.

"And Chandra's Organized, Inc. does draw the line at

27

what it will do for a client?" he taunted, breaking the eggs into a bowl.

"There's no need to be insulting at this stage," she replied stiffly.

"I still want an answer to my question," he told her calmly, filling the copper-bottomed pot with water and setting it on the stove. "Why did the president of Chandra's Organized indulge in the client's margaritas to such an extent last night?"

"I'd rather not talk about it, if you don't mind," she mumbled, refusing to look at him.

"But I do mind," he drawled coolly. "You see, I think you owe the client an explanation in this case."

"An apology should be sufficient under the circumstances!"

"But I want the explanation. And don't try telling me you have a weakness for margaritas. I've watched you around alcohol before, remember. That night I insisted on meeting you after work to discuss the plans for the party."

She remembered the evening very well. After a great deal of patient argument on his part she had allowed herself to be convinced that he simply didn't have time during the day to go over the party preparations. He had, as he reminded her loftily, a business to run. She would have to agree to discuss matters in the evening.

Reluctantly Chandra had let herself be popped into the black Ferrari and driven to an elegantly casual Mexican restaurant, where it had been a struggle keeping the conversation on business. He'd made it very clear that night that he was attracted to her, the glacier eyes heating with a seductive gleam as he sat across the table from her and watched her animated face in the candlelight.

Oh, he had power, all right, Chandra acknowledged ruefully. She had known deep inside that evening that she should have refused the job of handling his party, yet somehow she hadn't backed away as she ought to have done. She told herself it was because he was paying well

28

for her services and the party would allow her to make other important client contacts, but there had been more to it than that. She should have listened to her own inner warnings.

But if she'd done that, she realized grimly, there was no telling how long she would have gone on thinking Kirby Latimer was falling in love with her . . . .

"Well, Chandra?" he prompted in that sandpaper and velvet voice. Sandpaper for the underlying command and velvet for the soothing effect that made it easier to accept the command.

"I thought you had everything figured out, Reid," she said wearily, rubbing the bridge of her nose in an attempt to still the clamor in her head. "I was Harry Templeton's mistress. Wasn't that how you had it summarized?"

"No games this morning, honey," he cautioned easily. "You're in no shape to play them. Just tell me what I want to know." He was dumping the eggs into the swirling hot water now, eyeing them critically. His apparent concentration on the food didn't fool her, however. He meant to have an answer.

She shrugged fatalistically. What did it matter if he knew the truth? And he was right; she was too weak to fight this morning.

"One of the people who showed up as your guest last night was the man I had planned on marrying," she stated baldly.

There was a sudden and dangerous stillness in him. Carefully, Chandra didn't look in the direction of the stove. When he spoke again she could hear the cold and distant menace in him.

"What happened?"

"He arrived with his wife. I hadn't known he was married. Simple as that. I guess I, uh, overreacted to the news," she made herself add with a commendable touch of flippancy.

"Which one?" he said gruffly.

29

"What?" Chandra blinked uncertainly.

"Which guest?" he clarified, each word dropping like a rock.

"Kirby Latimer, if it makes any difference. I don't even think you know him. He arrived with Harry's group." Had good old Harry known or had it been a surprise to him, too? Was that what he had been trying to signal to her when he'd come through the door with the others? She'd seen the wary look on his friendly face and hadn't known what to make of it. There had been no chance to talk until after introductions were made and by then, of course, it was much too late. Kirby, with his usual aplomb, had merely smiled and pretended nothing was wrong. At least he hadn't pretended not to know her, she thought ruefully.

"Latimer," Reid said almost under his breath. "The journalist?"

She nodded, unable to say anything.

"Are you sleeping with him?"

"That's none of your damn business!"

"I want to know exactly where I stand!" he rasped, dishing up the eggs with a suppressed violence that alarmed her.

"Off to one side!"

"Don't get flippant with me, Chandra Madison," he advised, setting the dish of eggs and toast in front of her with a small clatter. "I'm suddenly not in the mood for it. And when I'm not in an indulgent mood I can chew little girls like you to pieces!"

The threat in him got her attention, bringing her head unwillingly around until his eyes ensnared hers. He was angry but it was a controlled anger. What would he be like if he were to lose his temper? She thought unhappily.

"You have no right to ask personal questions," she tried stoutly, wishing the aspirin would go to work. Reid seemed so large and intimidating standing there on the other side of the counter, forcing the confrontation. She just wasn't up to this, she told herself with an inner groan. Some other time . . .

He must have seen the incipient rebellion in her expression because abruptly he reached across the counter and cupped her face between two rough palms. She could feel the toughened skin of his hands on her cheeks. The callouses must be a legacy from the days when Reid Devlin had worked his own construction sites.

"Answer me, Chandra," he growled. "How long has the affair with Latimer been going on? How long have you been sleeping with him?"

"Leave me alone, Reid!"

His hands tightened on her face and she thought the pain in her head would send her through the roof.

"Stop it! You're hurting me!" she begged.

"Tell me what I want to know, damnit!"

It was too much for her this morning. It seemed simpler to give him his answer. Mentally labeling herself a coward, Chandra told him the truth.

"I've only known Kirby a month. We aren't . . . that is, things hadn't gotten to the stage you're talking about," she admitted wretchedly, hoping he would now free her aching head.

"A month!" he exclaimed, sounding truly astonished. "You've been seeing him a month and you haven't been to bed with him?"

"I know that you probably wouldn't bother with a woman who dragged her feet that long," she hissed. "But Kirby is . . . was different!"

"Only because he was lying to you all the way down the line," Reid muttered, dropping his hands from her face and scanning her bitter hazel eyes almost curiously. "But I doubt that you would have been able to stall him much longer. He looked well and truly married to me last night, not at all as if he were on the verge of divorcing his wife. He only intended an affair with you, Chandra. He

31

wouldn't have waited much longer before giving you an ultimatum!"

"Unlike you, I suppose?" she retorted waspishly, picking up the spoon and poking at the poached eggs experimentally. She wasn't in the least hungry but paying attention to the food gave her an excuse not to meet the probing, perceptive look in his gaze.

"Unlike me," he agreed laconically, moving around the kitchen again to collect his own dish of eggs and toast.

She said nothing as he came to sit beside her at the glass counter. Out of the corner of her eye she watched him sprinkle his food liberally with pepper from the carved wooden peppermill.

Chandra tried a bite of food in the uneasy silence. Uneasy on her part, that was. Her host and former client appeared to be thinking carefully, something she didn't find at all encouraging. But he didn't leave her long in doubt about what he was contemplating.

"Well, that, at any rate, clears up the last of the nagging questions," Reid observed, munching rye toast.

"I'm so glad your mind has been set at ease," she mocked, staring at her eggs. The first bite had gone down surprisingly well. Maybe she'd risk another in a moment.

"That was rather clever of you, using Harry as a red herring," he went on politely.

"I didn't. I merely let you assume what you wanted to assume. I never told you I was in love with Harry Templeton!"

"But you were in love with Kirby Latimer?" he asked, sounding skeptically amused.

"You don't sound as if you have much use for the term," she commented dryly.

"Love? I don't. It's a false word. Worse than the term relationship. 'Relationship' is admittedly an ambiguous word that can mean a lot of different things to different people. 'Love' is nothing more than a soft, totally deceptive term used to cover up the reality of plain old desire.

32

It imparts some mystical meaning to what is merely a relationship based on sex and mutual attraction," he stated with clear finality. He capped off the declaration by taking another bite of toast.

Chandra turned her head to stare at him, surprised by the degree of shock she felt. "And the word marriage?" she whispered, hazel eyes wide.

"An institution useful nowadays only for providing children with an acceptable last name and an economic base. If there are no children there's not much point in being married." He shrugged.

"Someone worked you over but good, didn't she?" Chandra observed thoughtfully.

He flicked her a narrowed, derisive glance. "Don't tell me that's sympathy stirring in those lovely gold and green eyes. If so, I can promise you it's very much misplaced. I'm not an embittered victim of divorce, little Chandra. I am a realist. I didn't go into my marriage with the idea that it would last forever, and sure enough, it didn't. What I hadn't counted on was how messy the divorce would get. I made up my mind after that to pursue serial monogamy without the added complication of contractual obligations."

"Serial monogamy?"

"Contrary to what is probably your conclusion, I have no wish to get entangled in a lot of short-term affairs. I prefer to deal with one woman at a time. So"—he shrugged—"I'm monogamous when I'm involved in a relationship. Which," he added rather pointedly, "is more than can be said for your Kirby Latimer!"

"You're quite the paragon of honesty, aren't you, Reid?" she flung back, stung.

"I shall probably give you a lot of reasons to call me a lot of things, Chandra, but dishonest isn't going to be one of them!" he vowed. She was appalled at the depth of determination she heard in his voice.

For the first time, it struck her that she might have been

hasty in her assessment of Reid Devlin. Perhaps he didn't move in the fast lane. Perhaps he'd carved out a path all his own. The thought didn't soften her feelings toward him one bit. If anything, she grew more wary. An unknown quantity was always more dangerous than a known and understood one.

"Don't worry, I don't intend to waste much time calling you anything," she assured him fervently. "If you'll excuse me, I'll be on my way. Thank you for the breakfast and the aspirin," she continued primly, sliding off the white leather stool and glancing around abstractedly for her purse. She needed that. The keys to the Porsche were in it.

"Sit down, Chandra," he told her coolly, not moving from his own stool. "We haven't finished talking."

"It's obvious there's nothing left to discuss! I'll send you the bill for my firm's services tomorrow." She moved toward the living room on somewhat shaky feet, wishing she could remember what had become of her purse. Had she left it in the entrance hall or had she put it in the den. If only she could remember last night more clearly!

She didn't hear him leave his seat and glide toward her over the thick carpet. The first intimation she had that he intended to enforce his command was when one large, tanned hand closed on her shoulder, halting her progress toward the entrance hall.

"Your firm's services," he told her easily, "haven't been concluded yet. Come on, Chandra. Let's go out on the balcony. The sun will feel good. What your body needs at the moment is rest."

"I'll go home and rest!" she argued, having no luck in trying to twist out from under his grip. He was guiding her toward the bank of windows that formed one of the living-room walls. Beyond them stretched a well-designed balcony, with a sweeping view of the cliffs and the ocean.

"You'll do as you're told, little one. You're too weak to do anything else!"

34

He was right. It was easier not to fight. What harm would it do to listen to his cynical commentary on love? She could always shut him out and think her own depressing thoughts, couldn't she?

Ensconced a few moments later on the comfortable lounger, Chandra took his advice and, closing her eyes, settled painfully back to let the warm sun soothe her limbs. She was aware of him taking the seat facing her. When she shot a quick glance from under lowered lashes she realized he was sitting forward, elbows on his knees, his hands clasped loosely in front of him. She didn't like the serious and determined expression on his rugged face. There was far too much steel in this man.

"In case you haven't realized what I'm after, Chandra . . ." he started grimly.

"Oh, I picked up on that right away," she murmured sarcastically. "And I must say, it's very decent of you to still honor me with your honest desire after the way I was sick all over your lovely bathroom!"

"Chandra, I want you to be my mistress!" he interrupted on what she could have sworn was an almost ragged note.

"Mistress!" she repeated savagely. "God! How I hate that word! A kept woman! A man's toy. Where have you been for the past few years, Reid Devlin? We don't use words like that anymore. Not in southern California, the cutting edge of the new morality! Out here we like to imply a certain forward-thinking equality when we're talking about situations like that!"

"Use whatever word you want! You know what I'm saying," he retorted broodingly.

"No, I'm not sure I do," she replied roundly. "I do know what you're *not* saying, however. You're not saying things like 'love' and 'commitment'!"

"Did you have words like that from Latimer?" he grated with meaning.

"A low blow, Mr. Devlin," she sighed. "A very low blow. Yes, as a matter of fact, I did!"

"Then you know how much they mean, don't you?" he noted aloofly.

She opened her eyes at that, meeting his with the impact of landing on hard ice. "I know what they're supposed to mean, Reid, and the man who can say them with the same honesty you're so proud of with words like mistress will be the man I'll go to wholeheartedly!"

"The way you came to my bed last night?" he shot back grimly.

She flinched, a frown of uncertainty forming on her forehead. "What's that supposed to mean?" she hedged.

"Only that I could have been forgiven last night for thinking you were more than willing to come to me on my terms," he told her evenly. "You clung to me throughout the last part of the party like a limpet. All chatty and bubbling over with warmth and invitation . . ."

"I was only trying to put on a good front. I'd . . . I'd been struck numb by seeing Kirby with a wife and I . . ."

"And you let me think you were responding to my advances at last. Hardly a very honest way to behave!"

"For Pete's sake! I'd had too much to drink! You can't hold me accountable for my actions!" she protested helplessly, knowing full well that was absolutely no excuse. She'd made a fool of herself and there was no one to blame but Chandra Madison.

"More excuses?" he taunted.

"If you think I'm so dishonest, why do you want me for a lover—pardon me, I mean mistress?" she challenged.

He relaxed, hard face softening as he regarded her outraged eyes. "Because I don't really think you're dishonest, of course. I was only trying to make you see that your behavior was subject to a critique, too."

"You don't need to tell me that." Chandra leaned back against the lounger morosely. "I'm painfully aware of the

36

fact." Her hand went to her head as she tried to determine if some of the headache was fading.

"Why didn't you tell me about Kirby Latimer?" he suddenly asked quietly.

She flicked open her eyes briefly and closed them again quickly. He had that determined-to-have-an-answer look that spelled disaster.

"I thought that, since you were good friends with Harry . . ." she began slowly.

"That I'd be more likely to leave his woman alone?"

"I wish you wouldn't talk like that," she countered irritably. "Why do you have to view things so . . . so *possessively?*"

"It's the way I am, I suppose," he muttered without apology. "I told you, I tend to be monogamous!"

"In a serial fashion, that is," she amplified. "One woman after another!"

"Chandra, I know you're still harboring illusions of some great, abiding love but you should know as well as I do that southern California isn't the place for that kind of romantic dream! At least what I'm offering is honest and straightforward. That's more than you've apparently found before or you would have long since been married to your knight in shining armor."

She drew a deep, shaky breath. He was right, she saw with sudden, agonizing clarity. He was absolutely right. To give the devil his due, he was offering an honest relationship.

"You're either going to have to learn to see through the little white lies and the deliberately misleading language of the time and the place or learn to appreciate the kind of thing I'm offering," he pressed ruthlessly. "Until you do, men like Kirby Latimer are going to have a field day with you!"

"It occurs to me there might be a third alternative," she said through clenched teeth.

"What's that?" he demanded unfeelingly.

"I could leave. Get back out of the fast lane and head for someplace where people are still capable of genuine love and affection." Even as she spoke, the words seemed to glitter with unexpected promise. Maybe that was the answer. Get out of this artificial rat race and back to the real world . . ..

"Forget it, honey," he told her brusquely. "Things aren't that much different anywhere else in the country. We're just on the leading edge of it here. Might as well face the worst possible case situation. Besides, you've built a successful business, own your own condominium. You like the good life as much as anyone else. You wouldn't really want to give it up for some small-town businessman or farmer!"

"What makes you such an expert on me?" He was intent on devastating her this morning, she thought, feeling hunted. She had to find the strength to get out of this house, and soon!

"I've known you for over a week. A man can learn a lot about a woman in whom he's interested given that much time. You're smart and ambitious but you're also a very warm, very charming female. I told you earlier, you intrigue me. There's something infinitely attractive about that combination of intelligence and fire. Your main problem is that a part of you is still living in a fairy-tale world. As long as you insist on doing that you're going to continue to get crushed by the Latimers of this world. One of these days you might not bounce back as readily as you are this morning."

"Out of the goodness of your heart you wouldn't want to see that happen, I suppose?" she charged.

"Chandra, with me you'll always know where you stand. There won't be any hidden wives or girl friends lurking about in the woodwork. As long as you're the woman in my life, you can be confident you're the only woman in my life!"

"You have no idea how that relieves my mind," she

managed tartly, lifting her lashes to fix him with a cold stare of contempt. "Come off it, Reid, you're no different from any other man out here and you know it. Your approach is a bit straighter than some of the others, but it's still a selfish, calculated attempt to get as much as you can with as little commitment as possible. I don't want to hear any more. I'm leaving!"

It took every drop of energy she had, but Chandra made it to her feet. She thought she remembered where the purse was now. She'd left it on the small table in the den.

But even as she turned to negotiate a path back through the sliding glass doors into the brilliant living room, he was rising to block her exit. His hands came out to grasp her shoulders and she couldn't progress an inch against the sheer weight of him.

"You can't keep me here, Reid," she tried valiantly. Attempting a degree of haughtiness she was far from feeling, she tipped back her head to face him, eyes stormy.

"It's too late, Chandra," was all he said.

She stared at the implacable expression on his face, felt the unyielding strength in his hands, and was suddenly, coldly scared.

"Too late for what, Reid?" she got out tightly, telling herself she would not let this big man intimidate her. After all, if he hadn't taken advantage of her last night or this morning, he probably wasn't genuinely dangerous.

"I know too much . . ."

"No!" Her denial seemed to take him by surprise and Chandra realized with dismay she'd protested without thinking. After all, he couldn't know about her past. He couldn't possibly! It was four years behind her. All the pain and humiliation and trauma had been left behind together with the man who had caused it. Desperately she tried to recover lost ground, not liking the curious speculation in his eyes.

"I don't know what you're trying to imply, Reid, but

39

whatever deep, dark secrets you think you've discovered won't be sufficient leverage to get me back into your bed!"

His smile was a little crooked as he watched her face closely and, although his words were soothing, the speculation was still there in him.

"No deep, dark secrets, just a few insights. That's all I've been privileged to get. *Are* there any terrible secrets I should be aware of?" he drawled invitingly.

"Don't be ridiculous," she managed to scoff gamely. "I thought you were going to tell me that because you know about . . . about other men like Kirby you've decided I'm easy prey!"

That hadn't been what had panicked her for an instant, but she could hardly come out with the truth!

"Easy prey! You make yourself sound like a helpless little creature fleeing from a large cat! I resent that," he said, grinning.

"You don't see yourself as a cat?" she retorted, more than willing to veer the conversation away from her own secrets.

"Certainly not," he declared lightly. But the lightness didn't extend to his eyes. "I'm only a man trying very hard to talk you into an honest affair."

"You don't think your approach lacks a touch of romance?" she demanded scornfully.

"I'm hoping my approach," he said bluntly, "will seem like a breath of fresh air after Latimer's!"

"As I said before, it's different!" she mocked.

"It's straight," he corrected, his fingers kneading her shoulders gently as he sought to hold her eyes in a beguiling mesh. "Believe me, Chandra, you can trust me."

"For as long as the affair lasts?" she quipped, feeling the dangerous pull of him even through the fog of her hangover.

"If and when it ends . . ."

"Definitely 'when.' All affairs come to an end!"

"Regardless of the outcome," he began again, a hint of

40

impatient aggression in him, "you won't have any cause to doubt my honesty. Ever."

"Is that all that's in it for me? A man who will honestly tell me when he no longer desires me?" Chandra's hazel eyes gleamed in the bright morning light with the force of her disgust.

"I'll take care of you, Chandra." His eyes softened as he absorbed the impact of her feelings.

"I see you take a very old-fashioned approach to these things!" she flung at him vengefully, the tawny, sun-dried hair dancing around her shoulders as she tossed her head in annoyance. "Are you offering a carte blanche? Wasn't that what it was called in the last century when a man . . ." She paused, eyes narrowing. "How was it phrased? Oh, yes! When a man took a woman under his protection. I believe that was the euphemism!"

"Under his protection," Reid repeated slowly, clearly turning the words over in his mind. Then he nodded briefly, approvingly. "Yes, that sounds right. I'm offering you my protection, Chandra Madison."

He looked so confoundedly serious that she could only stare at him open-mouthed for a moment. "And the carte blanche?" she finally got out sweetly, wondering whether to slap his face or scratch out his eyes.

"A blank check?" He slanted her a glance in which humor was returning. "Well, within reason, I suppose. I might spring for a new Porsche to replace that poor, battered thing you're driving now."

"You're impossible," she sighed, realizing it was hopeless trying to use the sarcasm against him. It rolled off his tough hide like mercury out of a broken fever thermometer.

"I'm determined," he clarified, pulling her roughly against the massiveness of his chest and burying her face against his shoulder.

She felt his hands sliding down her back, molding her to the length of his hard, inflexible body, and wondered at his persistence. She hadn't been particularly pleasant to him this morning and after the fiasco of last night it seemed strange he should want anything more than to get her out of his house. The brief moments of laughter and fleeting instances of companionship they had known during the past few days while working together on the party hardly seemed sufficient to have aroused his interest. In any event, such moments had disappeared almost as soon as they arrived, burned off by the reality of who Reid Devlin was. A reality Chandra sought to keep before her conscious mind.

He was another successful, living-life-to-the-hilt, West Coast businessman who was obeying the California gospel to the letter, even if he was trying to be honest about it! What great virtue was there in honesty, she asked herself bleakly, when a man still wanted the same cheap thrills?

"I want to go home, Reid," she said quietly into the finely woven cotton of his shirt. She didn't have the energy to persist in this skirmish.

"All right, sweetheart," he agreed placatingly, rough fingers threading through her unkempt hair. "I'll take you home. But I meant what I said earlier, Chandra," he said in soft warning, putting her a little distance away from him.

"What?" she asked warily.

"It's too late to back out of this relationship. I've had you in my bed once and you're going to find yourself there again. Soon. It's where you belong. But next time," he admitted almost whimsically, "you're going to be very much aware of what you're doing!"

CHAPTER THREE

It was the ringing of the phone beside the bed that brought Chandra out of a sound sleep the next morning. For an instant her mind could only remember the previous day's awakening and resisted the summons but a second later everything fell into place again and she opened her eyes to the cheerful, wicker-furnished bedroom. Outside her window a palm-tree frond scratched familiarly against the glass. She was in her own bed, and her body, at least, was back to normal.

"Hello?" she mumbled sleepily after finding the receiver by sense of touch. Several odds and ends on the nightstand had been jostled in the process and a few now lay on the floor.

"When are you going to get this heap out of my drive?" The scratchy-soft voice brought Chandra wide awake as nothing else would have done.

"What's the matter, Reid? Afraid to have the neighbors think you're entertaining a weekend guest?" she managed spiritedly. She could visualize him sitting on the wide balcony, drinking his morning coffee and holding the white phone propped against his broad shoulder. Strange the image should be so clear. He would be wearing that little crooked smile that touched the corners of his mouth when he was amused, and the glacial eyes would be narrowed against the sunlight off the sea.

"My neighbors wouldn't give a damn if they thought I'd convinced you to stay the weekend but they do get nervous when the general tone of the neighborhood is being low-ered!"

"Is that a reference to my poor car's condition?" she grumbled, sitting up on the pillows and wondering why she was bothering with the banter. Why, in fact, the sound of his voice was not completely unwelcome.

"What do you do to your cars, honey? I don't see any evidence of a major collision but you look like you've taken it through a number of small wars!"

"Poor depth perception," she sighed obligingly, yawn-ing and glancing out the window. Across the lawn she could already see some early-morning risers enjoying the Sunday sunshine by the hot tub and pool complex the condominium owned.

"No kidding?" Reid said in surprise, sounding genuine-ly interested. "You mean the world looks flat to you?"

She gave a small burble of laughter at that. "Of course not! No flatter than it does to you if you close one eye! It's just that my eyes don't focus perfectly and I have a little trouble judging distances at close quarters."

"Like inside parking garages?" he suggested dryly, the humor in him plain.

"I also avoid parallel parking as much as possible and hold onto the handrail when I'm going up or down stairs. I am, to put it bluntly, a touch clumsy at times!"

"Was that why you hung on to me so carefully the night of the party after you'd had one too many margaritas?" he inquired kindly.

"You're no gentleman to remind me of that!" she snapped, her own humor fading rapidly.

"There aren't any gentlemen in this part of the country, little Chandra. When are you going to learn that?" he chided.

About to respond with a scathing comment, Chandra found herself holding back the words. It struck her belat-edly that, all things considered, Reid Devlin had acted with a kind of gentlemanlike behavior the day before. It

44

wasn't, perhaps, old-fashioned gallantry, but he had been patient and rather kind in his own way. She wondered how many other men would have been as easygoing about a woman who had collapsed willingly enough in bed and then failed to deliver on the implied promise!

But she couldn't very well say such things over the phone, so Chandra let the remark pass.

"So now you want me to remove my vehicle from the premises, hmm?" she murmured, sliding out of bed and onto the deep green rug.

"I'll be by for you in half an hour. We'll come back here and you can get your car. See you in thirty minutes, Chandra, and you'd better be ready!" he demanded lightly. "Or else!"

"Or else what?" she complained, trying to think of another way she could collect the offending automobile. Perhaps if she called a cab . . .

"Or else I'll help you get ready. You already know how good I am at that sort of thing!"

Chandra hung the phone up in his ear and started grimly for the bathroom.

Half an hour later the black Ferrari pulled neatly into the drive. Chandra, watering plants on the deck above, watched, unnoticed, as Reid uncoiled his large, lean frame from the leashed cat of a car and started toward her front door.

He was big, she thought idly, staring down at the dark brown head with its copper hints. Large and strong and . . . she sought for another word. Dependable? No, that wasn't right. The man had no sense of commitment, she reminded herself. He wanted to be free to enjoy the easily taken trappings of the good life. He didn't want the indefinite ties of a commitment like marriage. Such a man couldn't possibly be termed dependable, could he?

She wondered sadly what it was about him that stirred

her senses this morning. Was it the effect of thinking too much about the intimacy of the preceding morning? The memories hadn't given her much peace in the intervening time. And there were other memories, too. Memories that stirred just under the surface as tiny, tantalizing flashes of the night of the party returned at odd moments. Looking at him now, some of those images flitted once more on the fringes of her mind. The warm, infinitely strong arms that had carried her to the bed. The heat of his body during the night. The pleased satisfaction in his eyes the next morning, just as if she had given him what he wanted in bed. Forcefully, Chandra pushed the thoughts aside. One had to be cool and casual about this kind of thing. It was the only approach. Southern California machismo!

"Up here, Reid," she called with deliberate jauntiness. A jauntiness that came easily to her most days. "I'll be down in a minute."

He glanced up, blue-gray eyes clashing with hers as he took in the sight of her on the deck.

"Congratulations." He grinned knowingly. "You look fully recovered!"

"Other than the fact that I've sworn off margaritas for a while, life is back to normal," she assured him meaningfully as she tipped the watering pot over the last of the ferns.

He smiled but said nothing, waiting patiently as she went back through the bedroom and down the stairs to open the door for him. Face to face with him she lost the advantage of being able to look down on the man, and once again her body was curiously aware of the size and strength in Reid Devlin. He was wearing the ubiquitous faded jeans and open-necked shirt that nearly everyone in sight on the palm-lined street wore. But the style suited him in a unique way. It emphasized the flat, hard line of his stomach and the well-muscled thighs.

She could hardly find fault with his clothing, Chandra

admitted with a wry, inner grin, when she was wearing very much the same style. The chocolate-brown long-sleeved shirt she had on was open at the neck in a rakish manner that exposed the pleasant line of her throat and the single gold chain she wore around her neck. The color contrasted nicely with the tawny shade of her hair, which was back in its deceptively casual knot. Her hazel eyes, she had been relieved to notice, had regained their normal liveliness, and the curve of her lips came with automatic readiness. Her own jeans fit like a glove in the approved local style.

"This is a nice place," Reid noted politely, stepping into the airy, wicker-and-plant furnished room. He had seen her condominium only from the outside. On the night he had insisted on taking her to the Mexican restaurant Chandra had pointedly not invited him in. "When did you buy it?"

"Nearly four years ago," she answered, following his glance as he took in the patio-styled room, designed for indoor-outdoor living. "Right after I moved to California."

"Where were you moving from?" he asked curiously, turning to smile straight at her.

"Phoenix," she replied shortly. It wasn't a topic of conversation she wanted to pursue. She preferred to forget all about Phoenix. Deliberately she sought to bring the conversation back to the condominium.

"As soon as I arrived I got caught up in the real-estate craze," she chuckled good-naturedly. "Got involved with the usual panic everyone out here feels about owning property and scraped together every dime I had for the down payment on this place!"

"You did the right thing," he told her knowledgeably. "This area of San Diego county has appreciated nicely in the past four years."

"Hasn't just about everything?" she said, grimacing,

reaching for her leather shoulder bag. "I'm ready to go now."

She ought to offer him a cup of coffee, she thought fleetingly, but something made her wary of offering this man anything at all. It would be inviting a considerable degree of risk to extend that sort of casual courtesy to a man who was looking at her now as if he'd meant every word he'd said yesterday about giving her his "protection"!

Reid politely ignored the small rudeness, leading her out to the car. There was a tiny smile playing around the corners of his mouth, however, as he slid onto the seat beside her. Some warning instinct made Chandra frown when he started the engine.

He was backing the sleek vehicle out of the drive with a casual expertise Chandra envied when he said very calmly, not looking at her, "About your car . . ."

"Yes?" she prompted cautiously, not liking the veiled laughter in him.

"I'm afraid I'm holding the poor thing hostage for the day, sweetheart," he confided, his eyes finally meeting hers just as he was about to pull out onto the street.

"What are you talking about?" she demanded warily.

"Simple enough," he explained gently, guiding the car down the well-groomed boulevard. "Spend the day with me and I'll let you have your car back tonight."

"Reid, I'm not in a mood to play games. . . ."

"No games. A kidnapping, pure and simple! I told you, I'm usually quite straightforward in my deals. Anything special you'd like to do today or do you want to leave the program up to me?"

"This is ridiculous! You can't just . . . just kidnap me for a day! I want my car!"

"You'll get it. This evening. I thought we might go to the beach this morning and then have lunch at an excellent little restaurant I know that specializes in fish. . . ."

"No!" She could imagine what he had in mind. A se-

48

cluded beach and an intimate luncheon for two. "You're out of your mind if you think I'm going to let you . . ." She broke off, floundering, and felt the red rush into her face.

"Let me spend the day seducing you?" he concluded for her. "You might as well get used to it, honey. I'm going to spend a great deal of time working on the project and experience has taught me that if I apply myself thoroughly enough, I usually get what I want."

"A regular Horatio Alger!" she tossed back nastily, shooting him a ferocious glance.

"Definitely. I believe in self-reliance and hard work." He nodded agreeably. "Now, one more time. Any preferences or are you going to leave everything in my hands?" He quirked a dark brow interestedly.

She glared at him for a moment. He meant it, she thought worriedly. Her best bet was to take a hand in the decision of where they would spend the day. If she picked a busy, crowded place she could probably give him the slip and take a bus home.

"You'll agree to spend the day where I want to spend it?" she verified, one nail tapping with annoyance against the black leather upholstery. She kept her gaze straight ahead, not looking at him.

"I'm at your service," he chuckled. She could feel him registering the determined line of her profile.

"All right. I choose the zoo!"

"The zoo!"

She sensed she'd taken him by surprise and the feeling gave her a definite pleasure. "That's right," she replied smoothly. "I would like to spend the day at the San Diego Zoo. One of the world's finest zoos," she went on in a chanting, tour-guidelike voice, "with over five thousand animals, some of them the rarest specimens in captivity. These animals have been brought from all over the world . . ."

"Enough!" he interrupted feelingly. "We'll go to the zoo!"

He was as good as his word, Chandra admitted to herself as they drove through fourteen-hundred-acre Balboa Park in central San Diego that housed the zoo as well as several museums and an outdoor theater. Perhaps she wouldn't look for a bus right away. She loved the zoo. Discovering it had been one of the most exciting things that had happened to her after she'd made the move to California.

Half an hour into the visit, Chandra was munching popcorn and had put off the idea of finding a bus indefinitely. She was having too much fun.

"Do you come here often?" Reid asked at one point as they walked through the canyon and mesa complex that housed the animals.

"Several times a year. I haven't been for several months, though." She smiled, extending the popcorn sack politely. "Enjoying yourself?"

He helped himself to the popcorn with a large fist and his eyes teased her wryly. "It wasn't exactly how I'd planned to spend the morning, but now that I'm here, I'm enjoying it, yes. One can learn a lot from watching animals, like the peacock over there," he added studiously, indicating a quiet corner of the park where the colorful bird had spread his huge tail feathers in an effort to attract one of several hens who were patently ignoring him.

Automatically Chandra glanced around in time to see the peacock, clearly at the end of his patience, give up his polite posturing and simply grab the little hen as she wandered into range. Hastily Chandra looked away.

"Not the most gentlemanly of approaches," Reid laughed as he reached for her hand and wrapped his own around it, "but an honest one!"

"Honesty doesn't make up for everything!" she informed him loftily.

"It's better than a lot of false, meaningless promises," he said deeply. "Isn't it, Chandra?"

She resisted the urgent, coaxing expression in the clear ice of his eyes and wondered why it took such an effort to do so.

The day passed with a disarming ease that Chandra knew ought to be a warning in itself. But when dusk had settled at last and Reid, without asking, took her to a restaurant with a panoramic view of the San Diego harbor, she didn't protest. After all, she reasoned staunchly, she had to eat.

But when he at last drove her back to La Jolla, ostensibly so that she could collect the Porsche, she did give herself a series of bracing lectures. It wasn't that she was afraid of his next move, she told herself grimly. Like the peacock in the park today, Reid was still at the stage of trying to attract her without alarming her unduly. He had been disturbingly attentive and agreeable throughout dinner. She didn't really believe he'd resort to grabbing her once she was within range and forcing himself on her. It wasn't that she didn't think he might not ultimately be capable of a certain level of violence, it was simply that he hadn't grown that impatient yet. He was satisfied to know that there was no other man in the picture since the night of the party.

"I'll fix you a cup of coffee before you drive home," he told her firmly as he parked the Ferrari beside the Porsche and opened his door.

"I don't need any sobering up tonight, Reid," she responded with an attempt at being unconcerned.

"Pity," he sighed, taking her arm and leading her toward the house. "There were some definite advantages dealing with you in an inebriated state. The trick, I suppose, is to find precisely the right level of inebriation!"

"You mean one short of the point where I pass out?" she taunted in remembered self-disgust.

"But one beyond the point at which you're still feeling

51

feisty! Come on, little Chandra, the evening isn't quite over yet. I've still got the keys to your car."

"Reid," she began stoutly, "this has gone far enough. I'll admit I've had a pleasant day . . ."

"Well, that's something, at least!"

"But if you think it means I'm coming around to your way of thinking, you're wrong. I'll give you full credit for your terrific honesty, but that's not what I'm looking for in a man. Can't you understand?" She bit her lip in vexation as he ignored her words and shoved her gently over the threshold. It wasn't until he'd shut the door deliberately that he spoke.

"Your problem, honey," he told her huskily, his eyes raking her from head to toe in a suddenly possessive glance, "is that you don't know what you should be looking for in a man. What you think you want doesn't exist. There are no knights in shining armor waiting to make your fairy-tale dreams come true. But there are a hell of a lot of men who will tell you what you want to hear if it means a chance at getting you into bed. There may even be a few fools still around who think that what you want is what they want, too, but their approach is even less honest than Latimer's because both of you would be lying to yourselves as well as each other. Stop clinging to fantasies, Chandra!"

"And take what you're offering?" she scoffed, a slow fire beginning to burn in the pit of her emotions. The fire ought to be one of anger and disgust but she knew it wasn't. It was a reaction to the melting ice in his eyes as he stood there surveying her. Once again embarrassing memories of the night of the party returned. She found herself thinking of the curling hair that matted his chest and the enticing male scent of him.

"Chandra, what I'm offering will be good for both of us. Is that so wrong?" He took a step forward and she automatically backed away.

Her retreat wasn't from fear of him, she realized vaguely. It was prompted by something much more dangerous, something she didn't even want to admit. She was experiencing a growing uncertainty of her own reactions. She shook her head as if to clear it and lifted her chin with a formal smile. It was definitely time to go home.

"I'll take my keys, Reid." She held out her palm imperiously.

"I'll take my kiss, first."

When he moved forward this time, purposefulness blazing in his eyes, she turned and, with a fine nonchalance that belied the state of her feelings, walked crisply out of reach toward the balcony. The sliding glass door stood open, allowing the balmy breeze off the night-darkened ocean to drift into the room.

Sensing that he was following, but not rushing her, Chandra stepped quickly out on the balcony.

And promptly tripped over the steel runners of the sliding glass door frame.

"Oh!" The exclamation was instinctive as she reached to steady herself. Of all the stupid times to not pay attention to her footwork!

His arm was around her, steadying her before she quite realized how close he had been behind her.

"Are you all right?" There was genuine concern in his voice.

"I'm fine," she groaned wretchedly. "I told you: poor depth perception."

"Or perhaps just general clumsiness?" he suggested, grinning cheerfully as he continued to hold her firmly around the waist. He used his grip to twist her around in his arms so that she was obliged to meet his eyes.

"I prefer my own diagnosis," she muttered, instinctively wedging a hand against his broad chest.

"I like the idea of you having such an endearing sort of weakness," he went on outrageously, bending his head to within an inch of her mouth. "You're capable of putting up such a flashy front when you try that it's reassuring to

53

know there's more than one area in which you need protection!"

"M-more than one area?" she breathed, painfully, tinglingly, vibrantly aware of him as he drew her lazily nearer. She had to put a stop to this. The man wasn't merely flirting, he wanted her on a very fundamental level. She sensed it in the feel of his hands pressing into her waist and in the hardness of his thighs as he forced her against his body. The desire and the male determination in him was part of his very essence and that made it all the more dangerous.

"Well, you have to admit you do have another major weakness," he told her huskily. "Up until now you've shown abominable taste in men!"

Before she could rally her defenses to protest the accusation his mouth was on hers in a fiercely aggressive, demanding kiss that wasted no more time in polite seduction. Like the little peahen at the zoo, when the male finally tired of playing games and made his move, she was quite helpless.

"Reid!" she choked out, only to have him take advantage of her parted lips to thrust his tongue boldly into the sweetness of her mouth. One of her hands was crushed against his chest and when she tried to flail at him with the other one, he simply trapped it in one of his massive fists and held it captive.

"Don't fight me, sweetheart," he half-ordered, half-pleaded against her lips. "I want you so much and I mean to have you. Take what I'm offering. You won't regret it, I swear it!"

She felt the tremor in his body communicate itself to her and knew her own body was responding. How difficult it was to fight such flagrant masculine demand! The knowledge that he wasn't trying to trick her with lies and promises somehow made it extraordinarily hard to resist.

With other men she would find herself holding back, testing the ground and seeking to ascertain the depth of

54

feelings involved. But Reid didn't allow that luxury. He had told her exactly how involved he intended to become, leaving no gray areas or lingering hopes about the relationship he proposed. He was, she suddenly realized, as honest in his lovemaking as he claimed. She could not doubt the intensity of his need and desire in that moment. Or, she added despairingly to herself, the appeal of him.

"Reid," she gasped as he tore his mouth away from hers to seek the sensitive line of her throat. "You know this isn't what I want!"

"Isn't it?" he grated, tasting her skin with lips and tongue before taking the tiniest of nips. "I don't think you really know what to look for because your head is so full of nonsense and dreams. When you find out that what I'm going to give you is the only reality you'll want it as much as I do!"

"No!" Her single word of denial was an attempt to convince both of them that she would not release the grip on her very female dreams so easily. Not when she had waited and searched so long for a real and abiding love.

"You don't know, little Chandra," he whispered coaxingly. "You just don't know yet how good it's going to be between us. Let me show you. Let me put your fears and doubts to rest."

His hands moved on her slenderness, gliding down her back to the curve of her waist and beyond to the fullness of her hips. He seemed to be taking such pleasure in the feel of her, she thought dazedly.

When his fingers curved under the roundness of her bottom, lifting and pulling her into the cradle of his thighs, she drew in her breath with a great gulp and felt it lodge in her throat. For a second or two she was dizzy with the heat and power of him. His maleness seemed to surge against her, making no secret of his need and—God help her!—she could hear the clamor of her own femininity responding.

Lifting her off her toes, his hands anchored under the

contour of her hips, he suddenly moved forward with her, forcing Chandra instinctively to wrap her arms around his neck.

"Reid!" she managed breathlessly, feeling small and fragile against him. "Put me down!"

"With pleasure," he agreed throatily, the velvet nearly obscuring the sandpaper in his words.

A moment later he shifted her weight, laying her down on the white leather sofa with an abruptness that made Chandra's head swim. She opened her eyes in time to absorb the impact he made on her senses as he lowered himself on top of her.

"Oh, Reid," she wailed, with a soft cry that could have been either desire or despair.

"Say it again," he growled, burying his face in the curve of her shoulder. "Say my name the way you would call a lover!"

His hips were bearing down on hers, forcing her deeply into the depths of the leather, trapping her with a primitive ease.

"I want to see you the way you were in my shower the other morning!" She felt his fingers on the buttons of her chocolate-colored blouse, making a mockery of its rakish collar and style as he stripped it from her.

The groan deep in his chest as he gained the prize of her unconfined breasts acted like a drug in her veins. Unconsciously her fingers tangled themselves deeply into the rich thickness of his hair, clenching and unclenching spasmodically as his lowered his head and kissed the nipple of one breast.

"Please, Reid," she heard herself say and didn't know what she pleaded for in that moment.

"I will please you," he told her roughly, longingly. "Just as you please me. You were made for my bed, sweet Chandra!"

She heard the passion in him and something in her wondered fiercely how a man like this could be incapable

56

of love. Real love. He had so much to give, she realized in the depths of her. Surely he could learn to give love?

But that was her silly, rationalizing brain spinning fairy tales again, she told herself desperately, her fingers beginning to stroke the muscled slopes of his back as he caressed her breasts and smothered her in his power. He was right, she thought piteously, she was seeking something which did not exist. Especially in him. Hadn't he made it clear?

But there would be no terrible surprises or humiliating revelations as there had been with men like Kirby Latimer, a traitorous part of her mind whispered seductively. With this man she would always know where she was. The relationship would be an honest one . . .

Her small reverie was broken into with a shattering jolt as Reid suddenly, commandingly, thrust one thigh heavily between her legs, forcing an even more intimate contact.

The moan in her throat was stifled by his mouth as he once again claimed it, at the same time anchoring her wrists above her head. The action of parting her legs and chaining her wrists hit Chandra with an unbelievably primitive and raw impact and she reacted to the passionate capture with a heretofore unknown excitement.

"Yes!" he shouted into her throat as she twisted furiously against him, arching herself into his strength with a savage femininity that took her own breath away.

She faced, for an instant, the thought that this couldn't be her, and then she was lost. Helplessly she felt herself being swept along on a tide of previously unguessed-at need and desire, her body straining to answer the demand in his.

"I will make you mine, little Chandra," he vowed in a harsh rasp against the skin of her cheek as he used his weight to control the writhing struggles of her aching body. "And then you won't have any more doubts! There will be no more chasing the will-o'-the-wisp you call love. There will be only the reality of you belonging to me!"

Somehow, through the blinding passion, the sheer, unadulterated possession in his voice managed to penetrate Chandra's consciousness. Belong to him! She echoed his words in her head. Belong to him! Belong to a man who didn't know how to love? Who offered only a businesslike affair? Was that what she had searched for so long?

"No!" she got out on a startlingly fierce whisper. "No, damnit! I want a man who can love!" Her hazel eyes flew open, beseeching him, chastising him, defying him.

"You want a man who can make you feel like this!" he told her hoarsely, using his legs to still her struggling limbs. He transferred both of her wrists into the manacle of one of his hands, pulling them more tautly over her head and leaving her exposed and vulnerable to his gaze and to the ravaging of his free hand.

He used both without mercy, grazing a nipple with his roughened palm, and then canceling the small punishment with gentle fingertips. He stormed across the softness of her stomach with his lips, dropping tiny, heated kisses into her navel and beyond. His fingers yanked at the snap of her jeans and then prowled maraudingly, dangerously toward the heart of her soft, hot passion.

"Reid! Let me go! I won't let you do this to me!"

"You can't stop me," he grated, the glitter in his eyes a combination of fire and ice that dared her to cool one or warm the other.

He was right. She couldn't stop him. If he didn't cease of his own accord there would be nothing she could do. Chandra admitted wretchedly that she probably couldn't even fight him. Her body already yearned for the possession he promised. Fretfully she turned her head to the side, into the leather of the couch back, and shut her eyes against the reality of falling in love with a man who couldn't love her.

The thought shook her more thoroughly than even his lovemaking. Falling in love! She couldn't be that stupid! No, it was only physical desire. That's all it could possibly be. Surely love couldn't be this seething, raging emotion that swamped the senses and left them exposed on their most primitive levels!

"Chandra, Chandra, don't turn away from me!" he snarled. She heard the unexpected plea in his voice and felt his hands cease their delicious ravishment. "Look at me, little one! Don't hide from what I am and what I'm offering! Please!"

Slowly, not understanding, not certain she wished to understand, she turned her head back to face him with wide, haunted hazel eyes.

He looked down on the bruised lips and appalled gaze and his own lashes closed momentarily as if he sought to control himself. Slowly his hands lifted from her skin, leaving her feeling bereft.

"Chandra, I didn't mean to rush you. I know you're still clinging to your crazy fantasies."

He swung himself up and off the couch, pacing across the room to stand in front of the windows facing the sea. She saw the tension in his shoulders and part of her wanted to soothe it. But common sense prevailed as she slowly levered herself to a sitting position.

"But I can't wait indefinitely for you to face reality," he continued more quietly. She could almost feel him getting his will under control. The effort it clearly took made her lick suddenly dry lips. He had been so very close to getting what he wanted tonight. It must be asking a great deal of himself to pull back like this at the last minute.

Shakily she got to her feet, putting on and buttoning her blouse with trembling fingers. It was, she realized, asking a lot of herself!

"Chandra . . . !" He turned to face her, the determined glitter of his eyes visible from the several feet now separating them. "Chandra, I'll let you go tonight. I'll give you a little more time, sweetheart. But please understand, I can't let you drag this out indefinitely. You belong in my bed and I think you know it. If you don't find the courage to face that on your own, I'll have to force the truth on you. I want you and after tonight you can't convince either me or yourself that you don't want me, too!"

"Reid . . ." she tried and then stopped, unable to find any words with which to deny the audacity of his statement.

The unremitting hardness in his face softened as he took in the sight of her standing uncertainly across the room. Without a word he fished the Porsche keys out of his pocket and walked toward her.

"Go home, little Chandra," he murmured, putting the keys in her numb palm. "Go home and try to face reality. It's not all that bad, I promise!" he added with an abrupt flash of unexpected humor.

She bit her lip and then wheeled away from the strange combination of gentle amusement and passion in those ice pools. Without another word she headed for the door.

"Drive carefully!" he called out behind her, his tone heavy with meaning.

Chandra did drive carefully, knowing she wasn't as much in control of herself as she ought to be. But fortunately the streets weren't crowded, and keeping her speed down to a level that annoyed the powerful car, she made it quite safely back to her own lonely bed.

CHAPTER FOUR

"Well? How did our first attempt at organizing a party go?" Alicia Adams demanded the moment Chandra walked into the office of Chandra's Organized, Inc. on Monday morning. "Were we a success?"

If you only knew! Chandra thought fervently, hiding a wince. She smiled brightly at the fifty-three-year-old woman who acted as secretary and general second-in-command of Chandra's Organized. Alicia, with her windswept dyed blond hair, excellent figure, and attractive features, looked more like forty-three. She was on her third marriage, and the diamond on her left hand this time was the biggest one yet. Alicia was quite content with life.

"The caterers did a good job, we didn't run out of liquor, and everyone seemed to have a good time," Chandra told her firmly, slinging her purse into a closet and adjusting a few of the more flagrantly loosened tendrils of her hair before heading for the inner office. "I think we were a success!" Certainly the hired hostess had gone out of her way to please the client!

"And Devlin seemed pleased?" Alicia pressed, eyeing her boss guilelessly. She had said little about Reid's obvious interest in Chandra but her well-made-up blue eyes twinkled with amusement as she asked the question.

"He, uh, seemed reasonably satisfied," Chandra said carefully, turning away from the mirror with a small rush and walking toward her office.

"I hope so, considering the fee he was paying!"

"He can afford it. What's on the agenda today?"

Alicia pulled out the bound computer printout that resided on the bookshelf near her desk and flipped through to the current date. Chandra stood in her office doorway, waiting for the various tasks to be enumerated.

"Carstairs' wife's birthday. We notify Carstairs and make arrangements for the flowers," Alicia began, her finger running down the line of names and associated responsibilities. Chandra's Organized, Inc. had assumed many of the small or routine tasks with which her busy, fast-living, fun-loving clients didn't wish to be bothered.

"We've also got to start addressing those invitations to the Morgans' yacht party . . ."

"Good thing you took that calligraphy course!"

"Umm." Alicia nodded, pleased one of her hobbies had landed the firm an important client. "That should add some class to the invitations. Let's see, we've also got a couple of Afghan hounds and a parrot to feed and water this week. . . . How about if I take the dogs and you take the bird? I handled a parrot once before and nearly lost a finger!"

"Which parrot is this?" Chandra demanded suspiciously.

"The Hendersons'," Alicia sighed.

"I had that one last time! The thing's vicious!"

"But you're the leader around here! Would you send your faithful follower out to deal with something you wouldn't deal with yourself?"

"This is no time for philosophical discussions on the art of leadership!" Chandra hesitated and then, grumbling, reached into the pocket of her jeans. "Tell you what, we'll flip for it!"

Chandra lost. Her luck didn't seem to be running in good form these days, she reflected as she finally took her seat in front of the wide mahogany desk, one leg tucked under her, and stared absently out the window.

A few blocks down the street from Chandra's Organized, Inc. the ocean shimmered invitingly in the summer sun, and the breeze could be felt through the open window. She found herself wondering idly what Reid's offices were like. Had his ex-wife decorated those, too? Disgustedly she put the idea out of her head.

She had to forget Reid Devlin, she told herself bitterly, reaching for an account book. He had made his position abundantly clear and, she reflected wryly, he had also made her position, should she choose to accept, equally clear! The memory of his satisfied nod of approval at the old-fashioned euphemism of a woman living under a man's protection made her lively mouth twist in wry mockery. And Reid prided himself on being honest and totally straightforward!

But, perhaps, she admitted, tapping a pencil tip distractedly against the wood surface of her desk, perhaps that was really how he saw the situation. How many women, she wondered, had he thus favored? And what form would his "protection" take? She had a hunch it would tend to be exactingly possessive. What would the woman receive in exchange for what would almost certainly be the loss of a good deal of freedom? Reid's promise that she would be the only woman in his life for the duration of the arrangement? He would be generous, certainly, but somehow that only made the whole idea even more distasteful to Chandra. She didn't need money; she was doing very well on her own now. Besides, her pride would never allow her to be a "kept" woman!

His protection . . . Chandra couldn't get the word out of her mind. If a man felt protective toward a woman could he learn to love her? She shook her head in dismay. Reid was right. She tended to live in a fantasy world where love was concerned. How many more Kirby Latimers would she have to meet before she realized that?

But even as she lectured herself, Chandra knew it was hopeless. Some part of her would go on looking for a man who knew how to love; a man whose "protection" would be extended because of that love and not out of a sense of possessiveness. A man who was not afraid of a true commitment.

And that was not the sort of man one encountered by getting drunk and waking up in his bed! Chandra told herself savagely. And thank God, a small voice added, that she had managed to escape Reid's physical possession the night of the party and again after the trip to the zoo. She had been playing with fire yesterday, she realized bleakly. It would constitute disaster, indeed, if she allowed him to exert the full force of his power over her. Every instinct in her warned of the danger in following that path. She knew beyond a shadow of a doubt that making love with Reid Devlin could never be a casual or fleeting experience. She would find herself irrevocably committed to the man afterward. And Reid Devlin wanted no irrevocable commitments!

"Chandra," Alicia called from the outer office a moment later as she answered the telephone, "call for you on line two."

"Thanks." Chandra picked up the receiver, her mind on Reid. Would he continue his pursuit after last night? With a sense of dread mingled with curious anticipation, she forced a professional calm into her greeting.

"This is Chandra. Can I help you?"

"Hello, Chandra," said the coolly mocking male voice on the other end of the line. "It's been a long time."

The words made her blood seem to chill. Without any effort the voice she thought she had forgotten brought back all the humiliation and anger of four years ago as if it had all happened yesterday. She sat frozen at her desk and stared at the palm-lined street outside her window with sightless eyes. In her mind's window she was seeing Phoenix, Arizona.

"What's the matter, Chandra? Don't you know who this is? Surely you haven't forgotten your old boss after all these years?" The hateful voice made her want to throw down the phone as if it were a snake.

"No, Blaine, I haven't forgotten you. Or what you did to me." Her own tone was cold and hard, she was glad to hear. What was this creature doing back in her life? She had put him and everything else that had happened four years ago out of her mind. Made a new life for herself . . .

"Don't tell me you're still holding that against me!" Blaine Sherwood chuckled in clear amusement. "That was four years ago! I told you at the time business is business."

"Yes, I believe those were your words," she observed dryly, repulsed.

"Besides," he continued reasonably. "One of us had to go, and of the two of us, it was you who could most afford to start over. I had a lot invested in my career at that point. . . ."

"So did I, Blaine. But starting over wasn't the worst part and you know it," she whispered.

"You mean, having to get over me was the bad part?" he murmured with an incredible ego. "I missed you, Chandra."

"You should have thought of that before you got into your little sideline business of industrial espionage!" she snapped, goaded. "And, no, Blaine. I hate to break it to you, but getting over you wasn't the hard part. I managed that the day I realized you were going to let me take the blame for your spying. The hard part was leaving a good job and co-workers who had been my friends under a cloud."

"You know they never actually proved anything, Chandra," he reminded her bracingly, a touch of annoyance in his voice. "You volunteered to quit! I never forced you to leave!"

"There was no way I could prove my innocence and you knew it, Blaine. I was the perfect scapegoat!" she charged bitterly.

"It's over now, Chandy," he soothed, using the nickname she'd come to hate.

"You're right. Four years over. And I don't want any reminders. Good-bye, Blaine . . ."

"Wait a second!" he urged. She could almost see him turning on the charm that came so easily to him. His night-black hair and dark eyes were a perfect compliment to the sexy, handsome features. Tall and dark, Blaine Sherwood knew how to use his natural good looks and masculine charm to gain almost anything he wanted. And that almost, but not quite, included Chandra Madison. Of course, she reminded herself fleetingly, he hadn't really wanted her as a lover, he had only charmed her long enough to use her to take the rap for his own business crime. Another lying, deceitful male to whom she had been attracted. What the devil was wrong with her, anyway? Reid was so very right. . . .

"Aren't you even curious about why I'm calling, Chandy?" he whispered invitingly.

"Not particularly." How she had come to hate that nickname!

"Chandy, that's not like you," he admonished sadly. "Can't you at least be kind to an old friend who's new in town?"

"New in town! What are you talking about, Blaine?" she asked sharply, her palms growing damp at the thought.

"Simple enough. I've been transferred from the Phoenix office to the new one we've just opened here in San Diego. Somebody from the home office told me she thought you'd also become part of the great California migration and I found your name in the phone book. Chandra's Organized, Inc., hmm? Gotten out of the corporate world altogether?"

"I decided I didn't like being at the mercy of a boss," she informed him icily. "I like having no one to answer to

66

but myself. There's no one above me who can use me . . ."

"Chandy, Chandy, I never used you. We were friends and we could have been more if you hadn't panicked and run away to San Diego."

Friends! she thought almost hysterically. The man had hinted at marriage just before he'd pulled the curtain down around her ears!

"Go to hell, Blaine! I've got work to do." Once more she started to set the receiver back into its cradle and once again he stopped her.

"This work of yours, Chandy," he drawled warningly. "You've built a nice little reputation for yourself, I presume?"

"I can't see that it's any business of yours!" God! What was coming now? The man was a rat, but, as she knew from experience, a dangerous one.

"Chandy," he murmured with soft menace, "reputations are fragile things."

"I'm aware of that, thanks to you!" she grated unthinkingly.

"Chandy, I just want to see you again . . ."

"The answer is no!"

"Somebody here in the office knows about your firm. Says you have a lot of status-conscious clients . . ." he began slowly.

"What are you talking about, Blaine?"

"How many of your clients know about your propensity for industrial espionage, Chandy?" he mocked.

"Are you threatening me, Blaine?" she got out in a frozen voice.

"Of course not! We're old friends. I'm only pointing out that it wouldn't do any harm to be kind to an old friend. I've got your office address. I'll pick you up for lunch tomorrow. How does that sound? We can talk about . . . old times." With a click in her ear, Blaine hung up the phone.

Hand shaking, Chandra did the same. What was he after? She didn't delude herself into thinking Blaine Sherwood wanted her back so badly he would threaten her with ruining her hard-won business reputation. She wasn't that much of a fool or an egotist. No, Blaine had found an angle and somehow he was going to use his "old friend" Chandra to help him make said angle work.

But what could it be? How long had he been in town before calling her? Long enough to figure out a way to use her again? Blaine, she had learned back in Phoenix, would do a lot for money and power. She couldn't prove it, but he was particularly proficient at selling professional secrets.

Chandra bit her lip. With her access to the private homes and the personal lives of her clients an outsider might think she could also have access to a few useful business secrets. She shook her head irritably. Surely he didn't think she would . . . ? No. He knew how horrified she'd been when she'd been politely asked about her association with some suspiciously leaked bid figures. The memory of that humiliation made her shut her eyes, and she curled her fingers into a fist at her side. She couldn't prove a thing one way or the other then and there wasn't a chance of clearing the thing up four years later.

How was she going to handle Blaine Sherwood? How could she get rid of him? She was damned if she'd start over again or run away one more time because of that man!

"Chandra, line one," Alicia called cheerfully.

"Thank you," Chandra murmured, looking at the beckoning phone with horror. Now what? Blaine again? Nervously she lifted the receiver.

"Can I help you?" she managed politely enough.

"Chandra, love! I've been trying to get hold of you! Where were you all day Sunday?" Kirby Latimer demanded, just as if nothing had happened at Reid's party. Just as if he hadn't shown up with a wife in tow.

68

"What do you want, Kirby?" she sighed, rubbing her forehead to try to rid herself of the gnawing headache that was taking shape.

"I want to explain, love. I know you must have been a little surprised at meeting Monica," he said easily.

"A little surprised? Why, Kirby, whatever made you think I wouldn't understand about you having a wife?" she tossed back with commendable derisiveness. This would be the last phone call she took today, she vowed, until Alicia had vetted them.

"It doesn't change anything between us, love," he assured her, obviously not certain if she was serious or not. "What we have is something very special and . . ."

"And your wife doesn't understand you, anyway?" she concluded tartly.

"Chandra, don't be upset," he pleaded. "Think about how much we mean to each other. Monica and I are on the verge of divorce. That's why I didn't tell you about her. What would be the point? I didn't want you to feel guilty and think you were the cause of the divorce. It was a decision that would have been made even if I'd never met you."

"Thoughtful of you to keep that burden off my shoulders!" She might have been crying right now, Chandra suddenly realized, if it hadn't been for Reid. Somehow the thought of him pushed her feelings toward Kirby into the background, where they no longer hurt so much. It was Reid's kiss she'd awakened remembering this morning, not Kirby's. Chandra swallowed as that thought struck her forcefully.

"Chandra, listen to me, you're upset at the moment, but you'll get over it when you calm down and start thinking about us. Our relationship is too important . . ."

The word "relationship" did it. Chandra wanted to hear no more. She slammed down the phone with a strong sense of satisfaction.

But the momentary release of her anger and frustration

didn't last. The self-disgust came back almost at once along with the nagging worry of Blaine Sherwood.

Restlessly she got up from the desk and began to pace the floor, deep in thought. It was time for Chandra's Organized, Inc. to organize the chaotic life of its president and founder, she decided grimly. She had to get things back under control.

But it all seemed to be happening at once. It was difficult to sort out priorities and make plans when everything appeared to be collapsing in on her like a circus tent.

That wasn't true, she reproached herself. She had problems, but they weren't all insoluble. Hadn't she pretty well gotten rid of the Kirby Latimer problem? Nothing, she knew, would induce her to see that worm again. And business was booming. She was on the way up financially, she reminded herself, which gave her a definite sense of freedom. She no longer had to work with the threat of someone above her holding her career in his hands. She had made friends here in California and she was adapting very well to the life-style. With one or two notable exceptions, she added with wry honesty.

Then why did everything seem to be pressing in on her today? It was probably the shock of having Blaine call
. . .

"Another call, Chandra! Line two again," Alicia sang out brightly.

This time Chandra thought twice before reaching for the phone. "Who is it, Alicia?" she asked warily.

"Reid Devlin, you lucky girl," Alicia called laughingly.

Reid! Chandra reached for the phone with a sense of relief. It would be good to talk to an honest man for a change this morning! At least she knew exactly where she was with Reid Devlin!

"Hello, Reid," she said, aware of the small catch in her throat.

"I trust you got home safe and sound last night? No stumbling over the steps or colliding with a lamppost?"

70

His velvet and sandpaper voice came to her ears with a small shock of pleasure. He sounded quite cheerful.

"Amazingly enough, yes," she retorted with a smile.

"I kicked myself for not insisting on driving you back to your place," he groaned. "But, frankly, if I had it would have been me waking up in a strange bedroom this morning! Not," he pointed out meaningfully, "that I would have minded."

"You're too gracious," she quipped, unable to give him the lecture he deserved.

"Aren't I, though," he agreed placidly. "What are you doing for dinner this evening?"

She hesitated and he picked up on it at once.

"I thought so," he said equably. "I'll pick you up at seven. I know a nice Japanese place with wells hidden under the table so you don't have to sit with your legs all folded up on the floor."

"But you *look* as if you're sitting on the floor, right?" She couldn't help but grin.

"The image is everything. Four years here should have taught you that!"

"It has, it has," she assured him quickly, knowing she was going to let him talk her into having dinner that evening. He might not be offering what her heart yearned for, but what he was offering was open and aboveboard. She wouldn't accept it, naturally, but she was beginning to appreciate the honest approach. And it would be nice to spend the evening without having to think of either Blaine or Kirby!

"I didn't find your bill in this morning's mail," he went on conversationally. "I thought you might have sent it special delivery."

"We haven't sent it out yet because we're still padding it."

"If you think I'm going to pay for the time I spent curing your hangover . . ." he began with laughing menace.

71

"Mention that one more time and I'll find a way to double the total. Believe me, your tab is high enough as it is."

"I'll have to hock the Ferrari?"

"For starters. Where are you calling from?"

"The office. I've got fifteen minutes until a meeting with a client so I thought I'd call and make you feel guilty for having driven me to a cold shower last night."

"Reid!"

"It's all right," he chuckled affectionately. "I figure it won't happen many more times. I can survive until you realize what you really want."

She heard the casual confidence in his voice and tried to tell herself it was the same kind of confidence she'd heard in Blaine's and Kirby's voices. But it wasn't. This man was different. The other two weren't even in the same class as Reid Devlin. This man would protect a woman, not use her.

Now where had that last thought come from? She'd been thinking too much about Reid Devlin's protection!

"You're convinced I'm living on dreams that won't come true, aren't you, Reid?" she said quietly into the phone. This morning she had almost convinced herself of that!

"I'm convinced," he retorted steadily, "that you're going to be happy with an honest relationship. When you stop fighting and put yourself into my care, you'll forget your childish dreams." He was no longer smiling into the phone, Chandra knew. The gray-blue glaciers of his eyes would be warming, but the line of his mouth would be hard and determined.

"You mean the offer of protection is still open after last night?" she taunted lightly, searching for a cool response.

"It's still open," he confirmed. "Perhaps I'll be able to talk you into accepting it tonight. Do you go as crazy over *sake* as you do over margaritas?"

"Nasty man! I'll see you at seven!" Chandra tossed down the phone.

But she couldn't get the word out of her head that evening as she sat across the low table from Reid, the small cup of warmed sake in her hands. She sipped the alcoholic beverage made from fermented rice and waited while he finished making up his mind. She had made her dinner decision quickly, but Reid was still studying the menu.

Reid had requested the privacy of an intimate tatami room and painted screens shielded them from other diners. There was, as promised, a well under the low table so that one had the sensation of being properly seated on pillows on the floor without the awkwardness. She tried a sample of the exquisitely prepared raw fish that Reid had ordered as an appetizer and was pleased. The kitchen knew how to handle fish. The meal would be a good one.

The restaurant was in the traditional southern California style of elegant casualness. Many diners were wearing jeans, and ordinarily Chandra would have done the same. The uniform was accepted everywhere. But on a note of whimsy this evening she had chosen a sleek, low-necked cotton sheath in vibrant red. From the look in his eyes when she'd greeted him at the door, Reid had been pleased. He was wearing his usual style in shirts with the top buttons undone, but tonight the cuffs were properly buttoned and he'd put on a pair of close-fitting slacks that emphasized the leanness of his strong build.

"Decided?" she asked with a smile as he finally put down the menu and reached for his own sake cup.

"Yes," he chuckled, lifting one brow reprovingly. "You're a speedy little thing, aren't you? Do you always make decisions so quickly?"

She shrugged. "I'm afraid so. I take it you see yourself as a more deliberative sort?" she said, grinning.

"Except where you're concerned," he returned smooth-

73

ly. "I knew I wanted you that first day I came to talk to you about doing my party!"

She felt herself going red and wondered if she'd ever grow accustomed to his frankly sexual approach. The heated gleam in his eyes told her he knew exactly how she was reacting. She felt the tingle along her nerves and found herself thinking again how easy it would be to love this man. If only he could offer what she truly wanted.

Gradually as the evening progressed Chandra began to relax, pushing the bitter memories of her telephone conversations with Blaine and Kirby out of her head. Two hours later as she went into Reid's arms on the dance floor the word protection came back once more. She wondered if it was protection Reid had offered his ex-wife. The protection of marriage. Had she thrown his care in his face and gone off to "find herself," leaving Reid determined to steer clear of marriage in the future? But he didn't seem unduly bitter about his marriage. Just determined not to get that involved again for the sake of a sexual attraction.

Protection. Chandra half smiled wryly to herself as she felt Reid's large hand forcing her head against his shoulder. She could use a little protection herself these days! How was she going to deal with Blaine Sherwood? No, she wouldn't think about that right now. . . .

"You feel very good in my arms, honey," Reid murmured into her ear, his breath warm on her hair. "Come home with me tonight and let me show you how much I want you. Let me convince you to accept my offer. There will be no regrets."

She shivered under the velvet wave of his words and the pressure of his hand as he forced her body against his own. It would be so easy, she thought dreamily as she wrapped her arms around his neck and let him move her gently to the music. All she had to do was give up the dream of a loving commitment and take what was being held out to her.

But she knew the affair would be one-sided in that she

would be unable to withhold her love. And she didn't want to contemplate too closely what it would be like to give love without receiving it. Not to this man.

"If you're not going to come home with me tonight," Reid mused some time later as he drove along the ocean-front, "the least you can do is give me a little something to tide me over." He pulled into a secluded turnout high on a cliff overlooking the moonlit sea.

"Reid, I don't think we should get this involved . . ." Chandra tried to say as she grasped his intention.

"I've been involved with you for over a week," he chid-ed, reaching for her in the darkened car. "Don't you real-ize I'm just marking time until I have you back in my bed?"

She looked up into his face as he pulled her across his lap. She was trapped between the steering wheel and his chest. In his eyes she could see a reflection of the silver that danced on the waves below the cliffs, and it had a hypnotic effect on her stirring senses. She couldn't find any more words as his mouth came down on hers.

The kiss was a lazy devouring of her lips, a relentless but gentle crushing action that didn't cease until her mouth surrendered and flowered under the assault. When his tongue probed inward, his hand moved to unfasten the zipper of her low-necked gown. She tensed momentarily as his fingers slid gently over the silk of her breasts, seek-ing the sensitive area of her nipples.

She felt her heart begin a thrilling beat, but it was the awareness of his increased pulse that was so seductive. She sighed softly and wrapped her fingers into his thick hair as he palmed the tip of her breast.

"My sweet, soft Chandra," he breathed raggedly, pull-ing his mouth free of hers and stringing kisses along the line of her jaw to the tip of her ear.

"Reid!" She heard the moan and realized it was from her own throat.

He responded by letting his calloused hand slide with

tantalizing gentleness across one breast, into the valley between and up the slope of the other.

She twisted, seeking more of the warmth of his chest, and with shaking fingertips began undoing the buttons of his shirt. He groaned as she found the male nipples and she felt his teeth nip first her earlobe and then the nape of her neck as she turned her mouth against his chest.

"What is it with you, Chandra?" he begged huskily as she touched the tip of her tongue to his chest in a hundred little fiery kisses. "Do you feel safe here in the car, is that it?"

She didn't answer, intent on the flames she was igniting in both of them. She was aware of his hand sliding under her breasts and then down the curve of her hip, inside the red dress. His fingers began to clench into the fullness of her thigh and the roundness of one buttock, and the sensation made her gasp with pleasure and desire.

Perhaps she did feel safer in the car, a part of her mind observed distantly. Reid would pet her and play with her here, but when it came time to stake his final claim he would want the privacy and room of his own bed. It gave her a sense of control.

And the sense of control, in turn, gave her a feeling of power. Reid let her wield it for a time, apparently resigned to his fate.

Her restraint removed as memories of last night's kisses flickered in and out of her head, Chandra strove to deepen the excitement. She felt the hardness of him under her leg as it pressed against her, and with butterfly softness her fingers trailed down the coppery hair of his chest following the trail to the uncompromising masculinity barely hidden by the material of his close-fitting slacks.

"Chandra!" Her name was a cry of warning and desire as she touched him, and an instant later he had gathered her even more closely against him, his free hand sliding intimately up the inside of her thigh to the elastic edge of her lacy briefs.

She moaned again and her legs shifted with an uncon-
scious enticement.

"Do you want to drive me insane?" he demanded fiercely.

"Yes," she whispered breathlessly, tipping back her
head across his cradling arm and laughing up at him with
sultry hazel eyes. "Yes," she repeated.

"There's a price for everything, sweetheart," he warned
with exciting menace. "Someday you'll pay for this!"

"Will I?" she taunted.

"You will," he vowed, and his head went lower so that
his teeth closed ever so gently over one nipple.

She took the opportunity to kiss the back of his neck
and the side of his throat, delighting in the heavy male
scent of him. It combined with the leather of the upholstery and the saltiness of the sea air, creating an incredibly
heady combination.

He was provoking her now with little darting forays of
his hand and tiny, almost-painful kisses. She was no longer
sure which of them was trying to drive the other insane
and she wasn't sure she cared. Her whole body was coming alive under the sensuous assault.

And then, when nothing in the world seemed to matter
anymore except the feel of him and the essence of him,
light swirled crazily across the inside roof of the Ferrari
and the sound of another car's engine drowned the roar
of the waves. A vehicle had pulled into the secluded turnout. The sound of rock music filled the air as the other
driver switched off the engine.

"Damn it to hell," Reid muttered ruefully, surfacing
much more rapidly than Chandra.

"What . . . what is it?" she demanded dazedly as he
righted her and quickly zipped up her dress. She was back
on her own side of the car before she fully realized what
had happened.

"I'm sure the kids next door don't mind, but I gave up
sharing scenic nighttime parking places years ago!"

The Ferrari roared to life and a moment later they were back on the highway, leaving the other couple in glorious solitude. Chandra couldn't help it. The giggle escaped.

"Be glad it wasn't a policeman," she advised, vastly amused by his wryly twisted mouth. "Think how embarrassed we would have been!"

"Explaining oneself to a cop in a situation like that is definitely for the young. We oldsters deserve the privacy of our own beds! Besides, I'm not about to have some cop or teenage kid leering at you!"

Chandra gave her head a small shake to finish clearing it and then realized how protective his words sounded. It was nice to have a man feel that way, she admitted privately.

The small incident had completely restored the atmosphere to normal, she realized, rolling down a window to sample the night air. There was nothing like being startled to kill a heavy dose of sexual tension, she thought with an inner laugh.

There was a thoughtful silence from the other side of the car and she wondered what Reid was thinking. She wasn't left long in doubt.

"Come home with me tonight, Chandra?" he invited very softly, barely loud enough to be heard over the hiss of the wind.

"No, Reid," she whispered, and wondered at the regret in her own words. Had he heard it? "I . . . I can't. Please understand. . . ."

"Little coward," he teased, and she realized he wasn't going to push the issue. Perhaps he'd been satisfied with her incredibly rapid response tonight. He was learning how quickly he could turn her on and he probably was consoling himself with that information.

"It's only a matter of time, honey," he persisted after a while. "You know that now, don't you?"

But Chandra didn't want to think about that. She *refused* to think about it.

She didn't want to contemplate it—but how was she going to avoid it, Chandra asked herself later as Reid brought her to her door.

"Are you going to subject me to another cold shower tonight, sweetheart?" he teased gently, taking her key and unlocking the door.

She ducked her head, unwilling to meet the beguiling light in his eyes. "I thought you said you could tolerate them until I, uh, came to my senses," she tried to mock, stepping into her home and feeling him follow. She didn't quite have the courage to tell him he couldn't come in.

"Does that remark mean you'll be coming to them fairly soon?" he murmured.

"You're old enough to know better than to try and read hidden meanings into a woman's words!" she scolded, dropping her purse on the couch and heading firmly for the kitchen. "Would you like a cup of coffee?"

"Thank you, yes." He came to lounge in the kitchen doorway, his eyes hooded and watchful. She could feel the waiting quality in him again. He was so sure it was only a matter of time. How, she thought wretchedly, was she going to resist if he kept up the pressure of the pursuit?

The answer to that was far too obvious. She wouldn't be able to resist. The realization shook her so much she forgot to pay attention to what she was doing with the mugs.

"Damn!" she exclaimed as one cascaded to the floor, breaking in several pieces.

Behind her Reid moved, coming forward to settle two square hands around her waist and lift her out of the way. He was laughing at her.

"Here, I'll take care of it," he said commandingly, going down on one knee to collect the scattered bits of pottery. "You see how useful I am? Someone to pick up the pieces when you get clumsy!"

"I've told you, it's a matter of depth perception!" she said, trying to sound reproachful.

"Call it what you want. I'll . . ."

Whatever he was going to say was cut off by the ringing of the telephone. Chandra turned toward it automatically, lifting the receiver off the wall as she watched Reid cleaning up the broken mug.

"Hello?"

"About time you got home, Chandy." Blaine's voice mocked her coolly. "Have a good time this evening? Thought you'd like to know I've got your address. I've decided not to wait until tomorrow at lunch. In fact, I got to thinking about how much easier it would be to renew old times tonight!"

"No, Blaine!" Her voice nearly cracked on the words, and Reid glanced up sharply. Helplessly she looked away from him, glaring fiercely at the wall. Not tonight! She couldn't deal with Blaine Sherwood tonight. "I've got company, Blaine," she got out, hoping she sounded more normal.

"Then you'll have to get rid of him, won't you?" he ordered crisply. "I've done a lot of thinking this afternoon, Chandy, and I know just how you and I can work together."

"Forget it, Blaine," she bit out, feeling trapped between the awful voice on the phone and Reid's presence behind her. He was on his feet now, stalking toward her. She closed her eyes, trying to fight down the building panic. The horrible feeling of being back under a collapsing circus tent was there again. Trapped.

"You're not exactly in a position to give me orders, are you, Chandy?" Blaine observed. "I know too much about your past. Things I doubt you'd want your 'company' knowing, too!"

"Blaine, I . . ."

Before she could summon an argument to ward him off the phone went dead in her hand. She looked at it blankly.

80

It had been a bad day for phones. She watched fascinated as Reid's competent fingers removed the receiver and hung it far too gently on the wall hook. Agonizingly she lifted her eyes to meet his.

He was very large, she thought abstractedly as they stared at each other in silence. Very large, very strong. A man who could shield his woman if he chose. A man who was offering protection when what she wanted was love.

But surely, she thought with sudden decision, this man's protection was worth the false "love" of a thousand Blaine Sherwoods or Kirby Latimers. It couldn't even be measured on the same scale. She licked her lips and spoke very quietly, her eyes never leaving his.

"About your . . . your offer of protection. I seem to find myself in need of it."

CHAPTER FIVE

The words had no sooner left her lips than Chandra desperately wished them unsaid. But it was too late, far too late. She knew that beyond any doubt from the fiercely and possessively satisfied fire that blazed into life in Reid's eyes.

"Reid! No!" she gasped as his fists came out to clasp her shoulders. She managed a shaky little smile and tried for a laugh to go with it as the prison of his hands closed on her. "I'm sorry, I didn't mean that literally. I'm just . . . just feeling a little pushed at the moment. But it's nothing I can't handle, honestly!"

"No, Chandra, honey," he denied huskily, his fingers squeezing her shoulders as if he'd never let go, "I'll take care of it. I'll take care of everything from now on!"

She swallowed, sensing the committed intent in him and not knowing how to deal with it. The lure of turning the mess over to him was strong, especially tonight, after finally having accepted the truth of his effect on her.

"Reid, this is becoming awkward," she tried again in a reasonable tone, although it was difficult to maintain reason when a man was holding you like this, hungering for you with eyes of ice and fire.

"Don't you think you can trust me?" he urged, sliding his hands from her shoulders down the length of her arms to her wrists.

"Well, yes, I suppose so, but this is really a private matter, Reid, and I don't think I should drag anyone else into it . . ." she began weakly. It was such a struggle trying to deny him the goal she'd carelessly dangled in front of him a moment earlier.

"I'm already in it, whatever it is," he said with that crooked little smile. "Don't you understand? Whatever affects you also affects me, now. You're accepting my protection, you just said so!"

"Reid, I spoke quickly, without really thinking . . ."

"You acted on instinct," he soothed, his fingers locking gently around her wrists and pulling them around behind his back so that she was pressed helplessly against him. With her head tipped back, vividly aware of the strength of his body, Chandra looked anxiously up into his rugged features.

"Trust your instincts, Chandra," he went on in a beguiling, coaxing voice that touched her with warm velvet. "Trust me."

"It's . . . it's not very pleasant," she suggested brokenly, violently torn now with the struggle going on inside herself. This man was offering what she needed at the moment, even if it wasn't exactly what her heart wanted.

"That doesn't matter," he assured her softly, eyes raking her tense, disturbed face.

No, she thought a little wildly, remembering how he'd held her the morning she'd been violently sick in his bathroom. Unpleasant things didn't seem to faze Reid Devlin unduly. He took them in stride.

"Oh, Reid," she sighed, collapsing against his chest and burying her head in the material of his shirt.

"Tell me, little one. I'll take care of everything." With one large hand he stroked the nape of her neck in a calming, mildly sensuous way that was enormously soothing.

Perhaps if she just talked it out with him, Chandra told herself silently; got his ideas on how to handle Blaine Sherwood. Reid had probably encountered men like Sherwood before and he might be able to offer suggestions. And she could put the suggestions to work without actually involving Reid directly. Without, she acknowledged honestly to herself, committing herself to Reid's protection and all that it implied.

"I'll . . . I'll try and explain what upset me, Reid," she mumbled into his shirt, "but please understand that I only want to talk about it. I'm not really asking for help . . ." Her voice trailed off anxiously.

"So tell me," he said softly, and she thought she could feel him smiling into her hair.

"It's a long story. . . ."

"Are you pregnant?" he interrupted calmly.

"No!" she exclaimed in astonishment, lifting her head off his shoulder and staring at him. Then she smiled as he merely shrugged and continued rubbing her nape. "Would that make you change your mind about your offer?" she couldn't resist saying provokingly.

"If you were pregnant? No."

She blinked at him a little uncertainly. "That's . . . very chivalrous of you," she was forced to admit, surprised.

"There's nothing chivalrous about it," he smiled back a trifle grimly. "When I said I would protect you, the offer included everything that was important to you. If that meant a child into the bargain, so be it."

She shook her head wonderingly and relaxed a little, probably, she reflected later, more than she should have. There was undoubtedly some very primitive, seductive appeal about a man who extended protection to a woman and her child, even if the baby wasn't his. But she didn't have time to analyze the reaction she felt at his words. Instead she found herself encouraged to plunge on with the whole sordid tale.

Slowly she unwound her hands from around his waist and walked across to stand with her back to the kitchen counter, facing him.

"Remember my telling you I left Phoenix four years ago?" she said carefully.

"I remember."

84

"Well, it wasn't exactly by choice," Chandra continued with a rueful twist of her mouth. "I left, to put it bluntly, under what is commonly referred to as a 'cloud.' I was working at the time for an aviation electronics firm. I had made my way up to a position of administrative assistant, even though I don't have a technical background. I was, I suppose, a glorified paper-shuffler and general handygirl for my boss, Blaine Sherwood."

"The man on the phone just now," Reid stated coolly, and Chandra nodded reluctantly.

"I'm afraid so. You have to understand, Reid," Chandra went on anxiously, "Blaine can be very . . . very charming. He's good-looking and successful and . . ."

"And you thought you'd found your prince, is that it? Only to have him turn into a frog?"

Chandra couldn't help it. It certainly was not a laughing matter, but something about the worldly superior note of disgust in Reid's voice made her grin, and the grin turned into a small chuckle.

"Life must be marvelous for people like you, Reid, who don't make the same mistakes the rest of us do!"

"Oh, I admit to making mistakes," he countered, his eyes responding to her humor, even if his mouth stayed firm, "but I do try and make it a point to learn from them!"

"Which can't be said about me?" she grumbled, her amusement fading as she contemplated the fact that Blaine Sherwood was on his way to her apartment.

"You won't have to fret about it anymore," Reid murmured, lounging back against the sink, his arms folded across his chest as he watched her. "I'm going to take care of you, remember?"

"Reid," she said quite clearly, "I'm only telling you the story. I haven't agreed to accept your offer! A little advice, perhaps, but that's all I'm looking for at the moment!"

"Tell me the rest of the story," he instructed, ignoring her warning.

She sighed, thinking. "Well, even though I thought it was a long story, I guess there's really not much more to tell. Blaine was running a small sideline of leaking company bid figures. Industrial espionage."

Reid's gray-blue eyes darkened slightly but he said nothing.

"I, fool that I was, didn't even know what was going on. For some reason," she added with self-mockery, "I had the impression that his interest in me was based on the fact that he was falling in love with me."

"And all the time he was setting you up?" Reid hazarded grimly.

"That's about the sum of it. Oh, I wasn't formally accused, you understand," she told him dryly, meeting his hard eyes openly. What a fool she had been! "But somehow there just didn't appear to be anyone else who could have had access to certain figures at certain times."

"Except for this Sherwood character, of course?"

Chandra nodded wretchedly. "Except for him. The initial flap died down after the first set of figures was leaked, but when it happened again . . ." She finished the sentence with a shrug.

"You couldn't come up with a good defense?" She couldn't tell from the tone of his voice precisely what he was thinking and it made her a little nervous. Perhaps she'd been hasty in divulging the story. She'd never told another soul.

"There was no good defense except to point the finger at my boss, who was already subtly pointing the finger at me. I did try it very tentatively, but no one bought it."

"Eventually the pressure got too much and you quit?"

"Yes."

"You've kept in touch with Sherwood since then, though?" he demanded, the first hint of anger entering his words.

"I may be a fool, but I'm not a damned fool!" she muttered waspishly, eyes narrowing. "Of course I didn't

86

keep in touch with him. I haven't heard from him or seen him in four years, thank God. Until," she added belatedly, "he called out of the blue today."

"And again tonight. Where is he?" Reid asked with cool caution.

"He's in San Diego. He phoned me this morning to tell me the good news," she admitted unhappily. "This morning when he called he told me I was to have lunch with him tomorrow . . ."

"The hell he did!"

"Tonight," she pressed on determinedly, "he was phoning to say he'd changed his mind about waiting until tomorrow. He's found out where I live and he's on his way over."

"Now?"

"Now."

Reid straightened away from the sink with an almost violent action, one hand reaching out to grasp her arm and haul her out of the kitchen.

"Move, woman!" he snapped in a voice that didn't sound willing to indulge any defiance. "Get your toothbrush and whatever else you need for work in the morning and let's get going!"

"But, Reid . . . Where are we going? What do you think you're doing?" she muttered, astounded by his abrupt move to take charge.

"We're going home to my place," he told her brusquely, pulling her into her bedroom and giving her a shove toward the bathroom as he opened one of her drawers.

"Your place!" she yelped, grabbing hold of the bathroom doorjamb in order to halt her forward progress. She whirled to face him. "Reid, I'm not going anywhere! I'm staying right here!" Confused and alarmed at his take-charge attitude, she glared at him as he pulled underwear from the drawer he'd opened.

"Honey, if there's one thing I've learned in life, it's that you don't let the enemy meet you on grounds of his choice.

87

You control the time and the place if at all possible. I want to be properly armed and ready when the confrontation comes . . ."

"Armed!" Chandra stared at him, shocked.

"Figuratively speaking," he assured her, seeing the stunned look on her face. "I want to know more about him and his background before I make a decision on how to handle him. That means I need a little time. Understand?"

"There's no need to get impatient with me, Reid Devlin," she stormed. "This is my problem, not yours! I told you, I was only asking for a bit of advice!"

"Well, the advice is to get your toothbrush and come with me! Now move, lady, or you'll find yourself having to borrow mine!"

Still Chandra hesitated. It was tempting to flee with this man and avoid having to confront Blaine Sherwood tonight. But what would Reid be expecting in return? She'd made it clear she was not accepting his offer, but did Reid understand that? He had avoided acknowledging her repeated denial, and a faint warning clicked in her mind.

Suddenly it was too late to argue. He was advancing toward her, the few clothes he'd packed in a paper bag that was dangling from one large hand.

"Ready?" he challenged, knowing very well she was not.

Chandra, torn between not wanting to really confront Blaine Sherwood and the nagging warning she felt about Reid's actions, gave up the contest. Whatever else he was, Reid was not at all like Blaine Sherwood, and at the moment that seemed to make him very much the lesser of two evils.

Without a word she turned back into the bathroom and grabbed her toothbrush.

A few minutes later she was stuffed gently into the Ferrari and Reid was backing out of her drive with his usual enviable ease. It must be nice to have a proper sense of distance, Chandra found herself thinking inconsequentially. One could be so casual about things like driving and stairs and . . .

"What are you doing?" she asked suddenly as he pulled the car to the opposite side of the street and immediately doused the headlights.

"We're going to wait for Sherwood to show up, of course," he explained absently.

"But I don't understand," she wailed. "I thought you wanted to avoid him tonight!"

"I want to avoid the confrontation. But I also want a look at him."

Reid sat with both hands curled around the steering wheel, his body apparently relaxed but somehow managing to radiate the lazy tension of a large jungle cat as it awaits its prey. He wasn't looking at her, but at the street; then suddenly he was watching the approach of a sleek sports car as it cruised slowly down the street toward Chandra's home.

In a chilled and frightened silence, she watched as Blaine Sherwood parked, opened the door of the car, and started up the walk. She realized she was very, very glad she wasn't waiting for him inside. Reid's presence beside her became infinitely reassuring. He was right. A prepared ambush was a far better way of dealing with a man like Blaine Sherwood than a direct, unprepared confrontation.

"That's him?" Reid asked quietly, his eyes focused grimly on the man ringing Chandra's doorbell.

Chandra stared at the tall, dark-haired man on her doorstep and swallowed uncomfortably. "That's him."

He hadn't changed much in four years, she decided with curious objectivity. Blaine was a few years younger than Reid, but he was almost as tall as the older man. He wasn't, she realized as Blaine turned away from her door in obvious disgust, in the same shape that Reid was. Blaine had gone a little soft, she thought. Perhaps he wasn't playing enough of his beloved tennis. Or, her mind suggested calmly, she'd gotten used to Reid's hardness and Blaine merely seemed soft in comparison.

But regardless of the physical shape of his body, Blaine Sherwood was still the dangerous, underhanded, conniving man she had known four years ago. She could tell that much by looking at the face she had once thought she loved. How could she have been such a fool? A good man's face should have the blunt ruggedness that Reid's had, not the too-pretty, essentially weak look Blaine wore. With a shiver, Chandra forced her mind away from that line of thought.

"He's angry," she whispered as Blaine gunned the engine of the little sports car with savage impatience.

"Do you particularly care?" Reid asked, a corner of his mouth quirking upward in an equally savage amusement as he turned his head to glance at her.

"He can be a dangerous man, Reid," Chandra said quietly.

"You think I'm not?"

She stared at him for a silent moment across the short span of leather seat. "I think," she said very slowly, knowing she spoke nothing less than the truth, "that I'm glad you're on my side in this. I'm glad it's not you who just came knocking on my door looking for me."

Some of the savagery went out of his smile as the more familiar crooked grin took its place. "If," he said with heavy meaning, eyes flaring in the darkness, "I'd been forced into a situation where I had to come looking for you, I sure as hell wouldn't have given you the advance warning Sherwood did! You wouldn't have had a chance to sneak away into the night!"

"Blaine was always fond of a little drama," she explained uncomfortably.

"And," Reid asserted briefly as he started the car's engine, "he was working under the assumption you were alone and unprotected."

Chandra couldn't think of a logical response to that, so

she said a little too brightly instead, "We don't have to go to your place now, Reid. He's gone. I can go home."

"No." The single word was unequivocal. "For two reasons," he added by way of explanation.

"Which are?" she charged, regaining her courage as the danger of Blaine's presence passed. Reid was already guiding the Ferrari into the street and she had a distinct feeling of being carried helplessly toward her destiny. But one had to put up some fight!

"Reason number one is that he'll likely be back in an hour or so after he's decided you've had a chance to sneak home. . . ."

"And reason number two?" Chandra's voice was brittle.

"Reason number two, naturally, is that the bargain's been made, honey," Reid said quietly but with total conviction. "You accepted my protection tonight. I'm not going to let you back out of the arrangement."

"Reid! I told you . . . !" she began agitatedly as her home slipped away behind the Ferrari, lost in the distance as the powerful car gathered speed.

"I know what you told me," he said flatly. "But the facts remain the same. You're mine now, Chandra. You became mine, whether you knew it or not, the night I carried you off to my bed after that party. Tonight I'm merely pulling in the reins."

"If you think I'm going to let you just . . . just take me home to bed with you, you're crazy!" she got out violently, not liking the strange mixture of feelings that were severely weakening her ability to put up any kind of fight against him. Good heavens! She was on the edge of falling in love with the man. Perhaps she'd already slipped over into the chasm awaiting her. How did a woman fight that?

"It's done, Chandra," he said soothingly as he piloted the car through the night. "There's no point in struggling now. It's too late for that. Stop running around in little nervous circles and relax. I'm going to take care of you."

"But you don't love me!" she cried, falling back on the one bitter, incontestable fact that made the situation so hard for her to accept.

"It's time you stopped looking for your fairy-tale knight, little one. I'm going to show you that reality is much more secure," he murmured, his eyes on the road. "I'll make you happy, Chandra. A hell of a lot happier than men like Sherwood and Latimer have made you!"

"You certainly aren't taking any chances that I'll mistake you for my knight in shining armor, are you, Reid?" she flung back, her eyes on his hard profile. "A *real* knight would render the service without demanding anything in return!"

"Then he'd be a fool, wouldn't he?" Reid observed easily.

"And," Chandra went on recklessly, goaded, "because he didn't demand anything in return I would probably have thrown myself into his arms out of gratitude and love!"

"No kidding?" She heard the laughter in his voice and acknowledged the hopelessness of trying to get him to change his mind. "I hadn't thought of that angle," he admitted.

"Perhaps you should try it. Who knows how I'll react?" she suggested, disgusted with herself for the hint of banter in her own voice. What was the matter with her? This was serious!

"But that would be dishonest of me, wouldn't it?" he charged softly.

"Dishonest?"

"Certainly. If I were to perform the service with an ulterior motive that I didn't reveal to you, I'd call that dishonest."

She groaned. "You would."

"I've told you before, I'm no gentleman, but I am honest!"

"Being honest does not give you an excuse to do anything you want!"

His mouth softened in the reflected light of the dash. "Tonight I will make it a point to give you what you want, honey."

She nibbled on her lower lip and considered that. She knew what he meant, of course, but she wondered if he'd really thought it out that well. She remembered how he'd carried her off to bed the night of the party but had stopped short of taking advantage of her. The next morning, he'd been solicitous of her, even gentle.

Her brain scurried on, recalling the way he had backed off the night before, after he'd spent the day with her at the zoo. He could have finished what he'd started and she wouldn't have been able to rebuke him later. He knew she was responding to him.

But still he'd halted when she'd tried to turn away from him. He hadn't pushed her. Deliberately Chandra let the evidence accumulate.

"What are you thinking about?" he broke into her thoughts to demand at one point.

"About Blaine," she lied. The truth was, she was coming to a few rapid but satisfying conclusions.

"Don't worry about him, sweetheart. I'll take care of him. You have my word."

"What are you going to do?" she asked as they neared their destination.

"I'm not sure yet, but I guarantee I'll find something effective."

She ignored that as he parked the car and came around to open her door.

Without a word he walked her toward the front door, and she thought his fingers trembled very slightly as he opened it. Telling herself she must have been mistaken, she sailed boldly past him into the white and chrome living room.

When she turned to smile at him, confident now of her

inner reasoning, Chandra found him leaning with his back against the door, hands behind him on the knob. He was studying her with a strangely hooded gaze.

"Now it's my turn to ask what you're thinking," she said almost lightly, her hazel eyes lively with confidence and warmth. Reid Devlin might not think of himself as such, but, in a rough and primitive sort of fashion, he was a gentleman. She could have his protection and all the time she wanted before fulfilling her end of the agreement. She knew that now.

"I'm thinking," he said, the sandpaper and velvet voice abruptly husky and thick. "That I've finally got you where I want you and I'm shaking like a schoolboy on his first date. If I let go of the door I might not make it across the room without falling down!"

"Oh, Reid!" she whispered. And in that moment she knew she had, indeed, stepped over the brink and fallen into the chasm of love. It became blindingly imperative that she drag him over the edge with her.

She walked toward him and he watched her approach from beneath lowered lashes. Chandra halted a few steps away and smiled at him again, hoping her own love didn't show. It was much too early for that kind of revelation. Reid Devlin wanted no part of love at this point. Or so he thought.

"I didn't think," she teased very softly, not knowing where the deep feminine mischief sprang from—perhaps it was a function of her growing self-confidence—"that it was ever difficult for a man. Especially not a man like you."

"It's not exactly easy on a man to want a woman as badly as I want you," he grated heavily.

Unable to stop herself, Chandra put out a hand and touched his hard, tanned cheek with her fingertips, feeling a small muscle work in his jaw as he swallowed. Her confidence soared. Reid might not be a victim of love, but

94

he was definitely a victim of passion. In a strange kind of way he was now at her mercy. She felt suddenly very womanly and wise.

He turned his lips into the vulnerable center of her palm and kissed her there. She could feel the trembling in him and smiled again.

"You don't know what it did to me to have to let you go home the morning after you'd spent the night here," he muttered throatily, his lips moving against her palm. "And last night . . . I don't know how I stopped last night!"

"The same way you'll stop tonight," she assured him gently.

His lashes lifted and she felt the tension in him as he met her eyes. She saw what she hadn't seen a moment ago in those gray and blue pools; what the dark lashes had been concealing. It was hunger. A raw and primitive and naked hunger. Some of her confidence ebbed as she lowered her hand with a hint of uncertainty.

"What are you talking about?" he whispered hoarsely.

She took a deep breath. "You're a fraud, Reid Devlin. You may be a bit rough around the edges, but you're basically a gentleman. Perhaps even a knight in shining armor!" She tried to end the sentence lightly but wasn't sure she succeeded. The tension was growing into a palpable sensation around her. "You won't force the bargain!"

"My poor, foolish Chandra," Reid growled almost harshly as he stepped unexpectedly away from the door and caught her face between his hands. "Still living in your fairy-tale world!"

"Reid, please!" she began, feeling the trembling in him again but knowing it wasn't just caused by passion this time. There was anger in him now and a surging male dominance that overwhelmed her senses.

"Tonight the fairy tales come to an end, Chandra Madison. Tonight you will become my woman! My mistress!"

95

he clarified with appalling satisfaction. "You're going to belong to me and by tomorrow morning you'll have stopped dreaming of your knight in shining armor. You're going to accept the reality of our relationship. You're going to accept my protection!"

CHAPTER SIX

Chandra stared up at him, eyes wide with the shock of his action. She'd convinced herself that he wouldn't force the issue and that she could handle him. She'd convinced herself that, deep down, Reid Devlin was her gentleman knight. How could she have been so stupid?

"Don't threaten me, Reid," she said tersely, trying to maintain some semblance of being in control of the situation. "We both know you're not going to hurt me."

"Agreed," he retorted gruffly, his rough palms tightening around her face as he lowered his head deliberately, "I'm not going to hurt you. I'm going to make you mine!"

Chandra's mouth parted for another argument but he sealed the words deep in her throat. Holding her head in the trap of his hands he thrust his tongue aggressively into her mouth, challenging and then taking the warmth he found there.

She was wrong, Chandra realized dizzily; her body hadn't completely recovered from the lovemaking earlier in the car. In spite of the intervening events, the flames leaped back to life with such urgency that she knew they could only have been a short distance below the surface, not extinguished.

Desperately she sank her fingers into the muscles of his chest, trying to break his grip, but Reid seemed oblivious of the effort. Inside her mouth, his tongue raged against her softness, reveling in it.

"Chandra, my little one, it's all over. Don't you understand?" he grated against her lips as his fingers moved upward to destroy the knot of her tawny hair. "There's no reason to fight me any longer! I'm going to take care of you and you've agreed to my care!"

"No, I never said . . . I only wanted to talk to you about my problem, I didn't mean . . ."

"It doesn't matter what you meant. It's done!"

She heard the rasping triumph in him. Already his breath was coming in the deep, heavy pants of arousal, and her own were not far behind.

His teeth closed with seductive warning on her lower lip when she tried to wrench her mouth away from his. Instantly the female in her capitulated to the small punishment, reacting instinctively to the physical strength of his maleness. Left to its own devices, her body would seek to please and provoke him. She remembered her own aggression earlier in the car, inspired by some vague sense of safety.

But there was no safety now, no underlying knowledge that Reid wouldn't risk fully claiming her in the front seat of a car.

Gone, too, was the assurance she had felt about his basic chivalry. The man had never lied to her, she admitted wildly as his kisses became heavy, drugging things—she had lied to herself. She had told herself fairy tales once more.

Beneath the impact of his mouth, Chandra knew she was weakening. Her lips felt bruised and helpless as he ravaged them again and again. His fingers were snarled in her hair, twisting and tightening as if he would chain her that way.

"I want you so badly, my Chandra," he muttered, licking the line of her cheek just below her eyelid. "I thought you were going to drive me crazy in the car tonight! I should know by now that every time I hold you in my arms, you drive me crazy!"

"But, Reid!" she cried brokenly, eyes shut against his

power. "You can't just . . . just take me as if you had a right . . ."

"You gave me the right," he said incontrovertibly but with gentle velvet overlying the roughness of his voice. "All you have to do now is trust me. Please trust me, Chandra!"

She heard the plea in him as his fingers moved over her shoulders and down her spine. As they slipped downward, they pulled the zipper tab with them. In a moment the red dress had fallen to her waist.

Even as she drew a ragged gasp at the knowledge of her own nudity, his hands, without pause, were following the curve of her full hips, pushing the dress the rest of the way to the floor.

She stood almost naked, wearing only the lacy briefs, looking up into his flaming, hungry eyes as he set her a small distance away from him, holding her by the shoulders. She shivered as the heat of the gaze swept her body but the tremor wasn't from fear. It was a reaction to the beguiling possession she read in his face and in every taut muscle of his lean frame as he surveyed his prize.

"Tell me the truth, sweetheart," he begged hoarsely, putting a fingertip to a pointed breast in a wondering, featherlight touch that brought the nipple almost painfully erect. "Would you walk away from me when you know how much I need you tonight? Would you walk away to continue your search for a fairy-tale hero?"

"Reid . . ." Her voice was a shaded, throaty cry as she waited with shaking tension for his next touch.

"A man in a fairy tale couldn't need his woman as much as I need you," he continued.

She was being hypnotized and she knew it, but there was nothing she could do about it. Since the morning he'd handled her so intimately in the shower her body had become attuned to his touch. She wanted more of him physically, even as her mind wanted more of him emotionally.

But where did the two meet? she asked herself as his hand on her breast lowered to draw lazy circles along the satin of her stomach. One thing was for certain. When he looked at her like this, touched her so hungrily and pleaded for her trust, she couldn't find the rational solution to the question.

She loved him and the acceptance of that swept every other consideration aside for the moment. She had thought herself in love with fairy-tale heroes before, but those emotions of the past faded before the overpowering sensation of loving this man.

"Come to me tonight, Chandra. For if you don't come of your own free will, I must surely take you. I can't put it off any longer!" he vowed.

His hands settled on her bare waist as he pulled her close once more, searching her eyes.

And Chandra surrendered without another protest. With a sigh of love and desire she wound her arms around his neck and lifted her lips for his kiss.

"Oh, my God, Chandra!"

He took the offered lips with impassioned need and then he lifted her high into his arms and started for the bedroom.

In the darkened room, its wide windows open to the sound of the sea, he set her down on the white carpet while he tossed back the bedclothes. Once more he lifted her and this time put her gently down onto the sheets, his eyes never leaving her moonlit body as he began removing his shirt and slacks.

She was aware of the slight fumbling of his fingers as he undid the buttons of his cuffs and the small indication of his inner agitation made her smile softly.

"Do you find me amusing, honey?" he asked with a self-mocking smile as he tossed the shirt into a dark corner. "I told you that you make me shake like a boy on his first date!"

100

"What do you think you do to me?" she whispered thickly.

"Tell me," he commanded as he came down on the bed beside her and gathered her into his arms. "Tell me what I do to you, my sweet Chandra!"

But she couldn't find the words beneath the furnace of his mouth so she told him with the soft, kitten moans in her throat and the fierce surrender of her body.

With a gentle violence that might have been prompted by love if it were an emotion that he believed in, his fingers tracked every inch of her from her earlobe to her ankle. And Chandra, knowing full well that her response was, indeed, prompted by love, arched into his touch and curved her fingers around the hardness of his thighs.

"Finish what you started tonight in the front seat of my car, my darling vixen," he growled, sliding intimate fingers along the inner softness of her leg. "I want to feel your hands on me, every inch of me!"

"In the car," she managed with a provocative, taunting smile, "I was safe. . . ."

"I can promise you there's no safety here in my bed," he retorted thickly as she teased the hair of his chest invitingly. His eyes burned as he drank in the sight of her hips and breasts touched with ocean moonlight.

"It sounds dangerous." Her nails dug lightly into the darkness of his nipple.

"It is." He touched her curving hip in blatant warning.

"Does your offer of protection extend this far?" she breathed as he peeled off the lacy briefs.

"There is nothing on earth," he swore as he lowered his head to trail kisses from breast to thigh, "that can protect you from me!"

"Oh, Reid!" The name was a gasping cry as he parted her legs with his hands to explore the secret of her inner warmth.

Her own fingers danced and clenched across the muscles of his shoulder and back, now reaching down to tighten violently around his buttock and now groping for the crisp hair of his chest.

She was lost in a world of incoherent words of need and oversensitized flesh. The whirling chaos of emotions had as its storm center the man who was generating the power that wrapped them both. A power Chandra no longer wished to fight.

She gave herself up to the overwhelming sensation of the moment, allowing her body to express its love on the most primitive of levels, and Reid took the response as if it were his by right. There was a possessive, claiming fierceness in him as if the need to assert his new ownership was paramount. Her series of deepening surrenders did not seem to satisfy him. With every new evidence of her acceptance of his mastery he pushed for another, more intimate level.

At last he had brought them both to the final edge and Chandra clung with helpless, willing abandon as he rose to settle his commanding weight squarely on top of her twisting body. For a moment he seemed to take a savage satisfaction in using his strength to gently trap her into stillness, and then he was storming her body completely.

In the end the timeless question of who had surrendered to whom might well have been asked. For even as he drove them both along the flashing path to fulfillment, Reid was as helplessly entwined in Chandra's arms as she was in his.

The final destination was reached with a shattering intensity that recognized no losers, only victors, and as it arrived Chandra heard her name hurled into the void as a talisman against the entropy of a chaotic universe. Reid was not alone in his primitive cry. His own name came from her lips with equal power.

For a long time there was the peace that exists between a man and a woman who have turned to each other in order to satisfy an elemental hunger. In the moonlit room filled with the distant crashing of the waves, Chandra lay in a damp tangle of arms and legs, unable and unwilling

102

to move. Her face was crushed against Reid's chest, his arm locking her to his side.

It wasn't until she whimsically put out the tip of her pink tongue and touched him that he seemed to rouse like a lazy lion after feasting.

"You are a wild little thing in my arms," he whispered in satisfied male amusement. "I shall never get tired of calling your bluff."

"My bluff?"

"Umm. Not that I don't enjoy the breezy nonchalance," he said, his chin on her hair. "But I especially like tearing it off you like a cloak and finding the passion and heat underneath! I knew," he added with deep pleasure, "that it was going to be like this. I think I knew it that first day in your office when I had to talk like a used-car salesman in order to get you to take on the job of organizing my party!"

"I'm surprised," she murmured dryly, "that having me pass out on you that night didn't put you off a bit!" She lifted her head to meet his eyes with a hint of laughter.

"A minor and temporary setback, as you've just seen," he assured her, his fingers stroking through the length of her hair. "But I'm a reasonably patient man . . ."

"Hah!"

"You doubt it?" he asked, looking offended. "Wait until you see how much time I give you before repeating that session we just finished!"

"How much time?"

"A good ten minutes, at least!"

For Chandra the rest of that night was a moment suspended in time. Again and again Reid reached for her in the darkness, as if he couldn't satisfy his need to possess her. And Chandra went to him with all the willing sweetness of a woman in love.

In the moonlit room she could forget the past and the future and concentrate only on the timeless present. The knowledge of her commitment was thrust to the back of her mind and only Reid's presence mattered, only Reid, until the morning light.

The sound of an alarm clock brought her out of a dreamless sleep.

The ringing of the alarm was followed almost immediately by a crashing thud and a muttered growl.

"Damn clock!"

Jolted awake, Chandra managed to focus blearily on an alarm clock lying on its side on the chrome nightstand. It looked dead.

She shifted her sleepy gaze to a grinning Reid. "You're a little rough on your clocks!"

"It's okay, I can afford new ones periodically," he chuckled richly.

He wrapped large hands around her neck and dragged her close against him for his kiss. The caress was a huge, lazy thing that spoke of remembered satisfaction and masculine contentment. When Chandra opened her eyes again it was to see the same emotions reflected in the blue and gray eyes.

"God, I wish we didn't have to go to work today," he muttered thickly, searching her mouth with the beginnings of passion. "It feels like we ought to be on a honeymoon, or something!"

Chandra froze, the magic of the night wiped away in a single sentence.

Slowly, with growing unease, she slipped out of the sleepy embrace and got to her feet beside the bed. Violently sensitive to her nakedness and the expression in his eyes as he watched her, she snatched the first toweling robe she found in his closet and wrapped it around her slenderness.

"Not a honeymoon," she forced herself to say very brightly, very breezily, with all the nonchalance he had said he found attractive. "Honeymoons are for people who fall in love and get married. They're not for people like us!"

She didn't look back at him as she fled to the bathroom and shut the door behind her. God! What a dumb thing to say, she thought savagely, sagging back against the door for an instant and staring at herself in the mirror over the sink.

But she'd meant it, damnit, she told herself, as she floundered into the shower and turned on the hot water. She was in love with Reid Devlin. She wanted to feel like a wife, not a mistress! She swore once again, more violently. Now she was using his word! Mistress!

She didn't hear the bathroom door open over the roar of the shower but a moment later Reid was climbing in beside her.

"I'd say this was one of those classic experiences of déjà vu," he chuckled good-naturedly as he picked up the soap and began scrubbing her back, "except that you look much livelier this morning than you did the last time I found myself in a shower with you."

So he was going to ignore her small outburst, she thought in resignation as she absorbed the feel of his strong hands on her back. The massaging action felt good, she thought wryly. She was aware of a definite hint of soreness in her muscles. Reid Devlin was a strong man and he'd not hesitated to let her know that strength last night.

"Shall we draw straws to see who fixes breakfast this morning?" he invited cheerfully as his fingers dipped below the end of her spine. He knew the most sensitive parts of her by now, she realized a trifle grimly.

"I don't usually eat much for breakfast," she managed with surprising matter-of-factness.

"I've got some ripe papaya," he drawled temptingly. "Doesn't that sound good? With a bit of lime juice? Fruit in the mornings, tacos for lunch, and something exotic at dinner. What could be more typically Californian than that?"

"Our arrangement!"

His hands paused on the slippery skin of her shoulders and he pulled her back against him. "I thought," he said very gently, bending his head over her as he pressed her against him, "that you'd stopped fighting me last night, honey. What's wrong this morning? I know you were happy in my arms. You can't hide a thing like that!"

Reid's hands passed down over her shoulders and skimmed lightly over her wet breasts to pause directly under their soft weight. Deliberately his thumbs grazed the tips of her nipples.

"You're not still worrying about Sherwood, are you?" he went on as if he'd stumbled onto the reason for her reserve all by himself.

"Oh, Lord! I've just remembered. He said he'd come by for me at lunch today!" And after not having found her at home last night, there was no telling what sort of mood Blaine was likely to be indulging. A dangerous man . . .

"Well, you won't be in the office, will you?" Reid said evenly. "You'll be having lunch with me!"

"Reid, I can't keep hiding from him! Sooner or later he'll find me and . . . and I think I know what he wants. . . ." Chandra concluded on a whisper.

"You?"

"No. I don't think he ever did want me. Not really. He only wanted to use me as a scapegoat. I have a feeling he's going to try and force me to work with him."

"How?" Reid demanded, dropping his hands and turning her around to face him. The sensuality of a moment earlier was completely gone as his hardened eyes raked her face. "How could he use you, Chandra?"

"If he's . . . still up to his old tricks," she suggested miserably, "I think he might expect me to do some spying for him. He knows about the sort of clients I attract. And . . . and he talked about the fragility of a business reputation. Oh, Reid, I can see him trying to blackmail me into spying on my clients!"

106

"That's nonsense!" he scoffed, shaking his head.

"You think so?" she demanded, unable to keep the hope out of her words.

"It doesn't matter one way or the other. I'll have him out of the picture by tonight!"

"Tonight! What are you going to do?"

"Leave it to me, sweetheart," he advised, dropping a kiss on her wet nose. "I'll take care of everything. That's the agreement, remember?"

"I remember," she whispered and then tore her eyes from his unself-conscious maleness and hastened out of the shower.

Half an hour later, as they breakfasted on fresh papayas and lime juice, Reid poured himself another cup of coffee and smiled across the low table at Chandra. They were sitting on the sunny balcony, enjoying the meal outdoors.

"We'll have to see about getting your things moved this week," he said calmly.

Chandra looked up warily. "My things?"

"Sure. What do you want to do with your furniture? Sell it?" he went on easily, stirring the coffee in his mug. His eyes met her frowning gaze.

"Sell my furniture!" she gulped. "Reid, I'm not moving in with you!"

"The hell you're not," he retorted mildly, but looking ready for battle.

"I'm a mistress, right?" she challenged.

It was his turn to frown. "Exactly right!" he muttered as if he weren't slicing into her with a dull knife.

"Well," Chandra got out bravely, "I'm not moving in with you. In case you didn't know, Reid Devlin, it's *wives* who share homes with their husbands! Mistresses keep their own homes! Mistresses," she concluded with gathering relish, "are a lot freer than wives!"

"What's the matter with you, Chandra?" he shot back. "We reached an agreement last night, damnit!"

"And I'm sticking to it, even though I was coerced into

107

it. But I'm sticking to the *letter* of it. I'm a mistress? Very well, I'll behave like one!"

"Women move in with men all the time!" he argued violently, his heavy brows drawn together in a fierce expression.

"That's different," she said breezily.

"What's different about it?"

"Men and women set up housekeeping together, with or without a license, because they're in love with each other. That hardly applies to our case! There's no rule that says a man has to love his mistress, only desire her. There's also no rule that says a mistress has to move in with him."

"You think you've got it all figured out, don't you?" he said roughly.

"I'm working on it!"

"Well, work a little harder," he ordered, leaning forward with clear menace, "because you haven't reached the right conclusions yet!"

"We'll see," she insisted with false nonchalance as she scooped out the last of her papaya and forced it down her throat.

"We sure as hell will!" he snapped and surged to his feet. "Come on, we'll both be late for work at this rate!"

In spite of his obvious annoyance, however, Reid did take a terse few minutes to instruct Chandra in what to say if and when Blaine contacted her. When Chandra returned to the office after feeding the vicious Henderson parrot, there was a note from Alicia to return Sherwood's call.

Taking a grip on her nerves, Chandra dialed the number on the pad in front of her.

"Running away isn't going to help, Chandy" were his first hateful words.

"What is it you want, Blaine?" she muttered, the receiver clenched tightly in her fist.

"A friendly chat, that's all, love," he assured her mockingly. "What happened last night? Afraid to tell your boyfriend you had another caller arriving? Did you go home with him?"

"Yes," she said with amazing calm. "As a matter of fact, I did."

"I know who he is, Chandy," he said slyly. "I was watching this morning when he dropped you off at work. I followed him back to that construction firm he owns and asked a few questions of some of the people who work there. He's a good catch, Chandy. I think he can be very useful to us."

"What are you talking about, Blaine?" she whispered, going very still. He'd followed Reid! Knew who he was!

"It's simple, love. When you work up the courage to meet me, I'll give you all the details. Better hurry, though, or I might lose my patience. . . ."

"And do what?" she rasped.

"Why, tell your rich friend about your propensity for light espionage, of course. I think it might take some of the glow off your relationship, don't you?"

"All right, Blaine," she said hurriedly. "Where do you want me to meet you? I . . . I can't make it for lunch. I have a client arriving."

"There's a lounge on Coronado . . ." Quickly he described the location.

"I know it," she said quietly.

"Be there after work, then. And, Chandy . . ."

"Yes, Blaine?"

"If you're tempted to run away again, think about what it would be like to lose your rich meal ticket!" The phone was hung up rudely in her ear.

For a few minutes Chandra sat trembling at her desk, whether from fear or anger, she couldn't be certain. Then, painstakingly, she dialed Reid's number.

She knew a light-headed sense of relief as his sandpaper and velvet voice came on the line.

"Reid?"

"What's wrong, honey," he said quietly. "Did Sherwood contact you?"

"Yes. He . . . he plans to meet me over on Coronado this evening after work. Will that work out with your plans?"

"Don't worry, it's going to be fine. What else did he say?"

"He . . . claimed to know who you were. Said he followed you back to your office this morning after you'd dropped me off at work."

"He did. Wasn't very subtle about it, either," Reid chuckled.

"I'm glad you're enjoying this!" she blazed, incensed that he should find anything humorous in the situation.

"Honey, Blaine Sherwood is turning out to be very small potatoes. I've already got some initial reports. By this evening I'll have all the ammunition I need."

He sounded so confident that Chandra bit her lip in vexation. "Reid?"

"What is it, honey," he said soothingly.

"You do believe me, don't you?" she whispered. "About what I said happened in Phoenix?"

"Of course I do. Why?"

"Because you're Blaine's first target if I don't agree to do as he says this evening. He's threatened to tell you I'm a . . . a thief! I think he wants me to spy on you or something. Maybe find a way to get information he can sell to your competitors."

"Hmm." Reid seemed to consider that prospect. "The best way to do that would be to move in with me, wouldn't it?" he finally suggested gravely.

Chandra held the phone away from her ear and stared at it. "Are you out of your mind?" she finally demanded, speaking into the mouthpiece again. "This is serious!"

"So am I, Chandra," he reminded her politely. "So am I."

She didn't know whether to laugh or cry. Shaking her

head silently, she murmured, "Thanks for believing me, Reid."

"It wouldn't matter," he said easily. "Even if I thought you were guilty as hell, I'd still take care of Sherwood for you and anyone or anything else that comes along. I'll see you at lunch, honey."

Chandra hung up the phone and sat looking at it for a very long time. A man's protection, she thought dazedly.

CHAPTER SEVEN

"Will you stop that damned pacing back and forth while you yell at me?" Reid complained several hours later. He was sprawled heavily in a fan-backed wicker chair, following Chandra's progress across her living room with brooding eyes.

"This is my house and I'll pace if I want to!" she snapped, whirling to face him with her hands planted in small fists on her jean-covered hips. "Be glad I'm doing something productive to work off my frustration over your high-handedness! I could just as easily be looking around for something large to lower on your stubborn head!"

"That wouldn't be productive?" he asked whimsically.

"I doubt it would have any effect at all!"

"Honey, I know you're a little upset over the way I handled things with Sherwood . . ." he began placatingly.

"A little upset!" she repeated, infuriated. "I'm enraged! I'm madder than hell! I'm . . ." Words failed her. She swung on her heel and resumed the momentarily halted pacing.

"How did I know you'd turn out to be such a bloodthirsty female?" There was the faintest lacing of humor in Reid's voice but his expression was carefully sober.

"You call it bloodthirsty to want to be . . ."

"In at the kill?" he concluded at once. "Yes."

"Well, I don't! I had a right to be there, Reid Devlin!"

"The agreement was that I would protect you, remember?" he said quietly.

"It wouldn't have made any difference if I'd been there to watch you protecting me! Damnit, Reid! I wanted to hear what Blaine told you! I wanted to be able to hear his side of the story. . . ."

"So you could defend yourself to me? Sweetheart, I've told you, I believe your side already. What makes you think I'd listen to Sherwood's version of events? What makes you think I care about what happened in the first place? All I was concerned with was getting rid of him. It's done. Let's forget it."

Chandra ground her teeth, coming to a halt in front of her patio windows and staring out into the gathering summer dusk. "I resent being pushed around and told what to do in the name of 'protecting' me," she muttered.

"Chandra," he said calmly, placatingly but with the rough sandpaper deep in his voice, "when we made our agreement, there was no discussion of details. It was assumed we'd each hold up our end of the deal."

"Don't you dare make it sound as if I'm trying to back out! Even though I never actually agreed to anything in the first place."

"In my bed last night you told me everything I needed to know," he stated flatly. She could feel his eyes drilling into the back of her chic maroon shirt, and trembled. How could she deny what had happened last night? She loved the man, infuriating and possessive and domineering as he was turning out to be.

"Then if you think I gave you my agreement last night," she challenged morosely, still staring out onto her patio, "why imply I'm trying to back out now?"

"Because now you're putting conditions on things," he muttered. "You won't move in with me; you don't like the way I kept you out of the picture while I dealt with Sherwood . . ."

"Perhaps," she suggested with grim relish, "I'm turning into a shrew. Perhaps you made your choice of mistress a bit hastily, Reid."

113

"I don't think I made any drastic mistakes there," he contradicted, and this time she could feel the humor in him. "I think the problem lies in the fact that my mistress hasn't had quite enough time to adjust to the way I do things."

She turned to glower at him, her hands clasped behind her slender back, feet braced slightly apart on the green rug. "What's that supposed to mean? That you're always this high-handed, overbearing, and dictatorial?"

"It means," he said very softly, watching her with his aggressive chin planted on his calloused palm as he braced his elbow on the chair arm, "that I think you need a little more time. That's all."

She stared at him uncertainly. "More time to get used to you?"

"Umm."

She tilted her head slightly to one side and eyed him suspiciously. "You're not going to push me into moving in with you?"

"Nope. I did a lot of thinking on the way back from Coronado tonight, Chandra." The glaciers of his eyes seemed very frozen at the moment but in their depths Chandra thought she still saw a flickering warmth. She prayed she still saw it. What was he going to do?

"Well, go on," she charged feistily. "Tell me what conclusions you reached." Had Blaine told him something awful after all? Something Reid had chosen to believe? This morning her protector had made it very clear he fully intended she should move in with him. Why the reversal?

Reid shrugged calmly. "I think, because I'm so sure of what I want, that I'm pushing you a little too hard, that's all. I'm proposing to give you some breathing room. You can stay here in your own home while you get used to the idea of living with me."

There was a strangely watchful gleam in those blue-gray eyes, Chandra told herself uneasily as she regarded him silently. Where was the satisfaction that had been there

114

that morning? Where was the steely determination to have his own way? Was Reid, in his own subtle way, trying to slide out of the arrangement? What *had* Blaine said?

Deliberately she sought to draw the cloak of nonchalance about herself. "Since I'd planned to live here, anyway," she said tersely, "I can't see what difference your big decision is going to make."

"I'm hoping," he said, rising with unexpected smoothness to his feet, "that it will make a very significant difference. Now stop glaring at me and get your purse. I'll take you out to eat and tell you all the gory details you think you should have been privileged to witness!"

Half an hour later, seated in the Polynesian atmosphere of one of the restaurants in the harbor area, Chandra made her usual swift menu selection and then waited impatiently for Reid to make his.

"Stop staring at me or I'll never get through this list of food," he grumbled, not raising his eyes from his menu.

"I'm not staring! For heaven's sake, Reid, hurry up. I want to hear everything!"

He sighed and folded the menu. "It's going to be your fault if I don't like what I'm ordering," he warned.

"What did he say when you showed up instead of me?" she demanded eagerly.

"I think he knew as soon as he saw me it was all over for him," Reid said easily, smiling at the waitress as she came to take their order.

Chandra was forced to bide her time during the small business, but as soon as the woman had vanished, leaving behind two glasses of wine, she caught Reid's eye vengefully.

"I hate to disappoint you, sweetheart," he told her dryly, "but it really wasn't all that dramatic. I told him what I had on him, warned him there was probably a lot more where that came from, and, uh, instructed him to leave you alone."

"What exactly did you have on him? You weren't very communicative after work today!"

"How could I communicate with you when you were busy throwing a tantrum in the front seat of my car?" he argued reasonably, eyes gleaming at her.

"I was not throwing a tantrum! I was merely infuriated that you intended to drop me off at home and go on to Coronado by yourself!" she informed him haughtily.

"Call it what you want, it effectively prevented rational communication."

"Reid!"

"All right, all right," he soothed, holding up a hand in a warding off gesture. "I simply unloaded on him everything my sources had managed to come up with during the day. It was probably just the tip of the iceberg, and he knew it. He knew if I really started digging I could ruin him with very little effort."

"But what was it you had on him?" she demanded again, trying to picture the self-confident Blaine facing Reid Devlin. It couldn't have been much of a contest, she thought in satisfaction. Reid would have demolished him.

"Well, to begin with, he's not in San Diego because your old firm transferred him. He's here because he was fired last month. Someone, it seems, finally realized what was going on back in Phoenix."

Chandra's hazel eyes widened. "He got caught?"

"I had that much information before noon. By five o'clock when I picked you up I had a lot more. He was involved in a shady Arizona land deal that is being investigated by the Federal government. He was also into fraudulent securities and a few other odds and ends. He's in San Diego working for one of the firms he bribed his way into by selling it your old company's secrets. I told him I was going to turn over everything I had and anything else I could find to his new employer if he didn't arrange to leave town rather quickly. Being fired from two major firms in a row is bound to make it difficult for him to continue operating. The gossip would travel fast. He elected to quit or arrange to get transferred. End of tale."

"That's all? A five-minute conversation and Blaine backed down?"

"Well, I did throw in the usual obligatory threat," Reid admitted calmly, taking a sip of his wine.

"*What* threat? Damnit! This is like pulling teeth!"

Reid lifted one massive shoulder in vast indifference. "I told him I'd take him apart if he ever came anywhere near you again."

"You did?" Chandra was momentarily entranced with the image. "What did he say then?"

"Conversation wasn't too coherent after that," Reid explained laconically. "He eventually left the parking lot in a cloud of dust. I don't think we'll ever see him again."

"You look very satisfied with the results," she observed thoughtfully.

"I am. He won't be back, Chandra, believe me."

"I do," she said quietly, a little dazed. And she did.

"Now about us," he began firmly as the salads arrived.

Chandra shook off her musing over the scene with Blaine and came back to the present in a hurry at his words. "Yes?" she tried to say casually.

"I meant what I said earlier, honey. I'm going to give you time." His voice was suddenly dark velvet and Chandra didn't trust it one bit.

"Why?" she said baldly.

He hesitated momentarily and then grinned self-deprecatingly. "Because there's not much else I can do, of course. Why do you think? I'm trying to make it look like the whole thing's my idea instead of admitting the truth, which is that I'm helpless in the face of your stubbornness!"

She slanted him a strange glance, feeling extremely wary. "I'm glad you've realized that much," she murmured, munching salad without tasting the honey-mustard dressing.

"I have," he proclaimed ruefully. "It's obvious you have your interpretation of the word mistress and I have mine. I'm hoping that, given time, I can convince you to accept mine."

"How much time?" she asked immediately, hiding her growing uncertainty. What was going on here? This didn't sound like Reid, at least, not the Reid in whose arms she had surrendered so willingly last night.

He frowned briefly, forking up his salad with an impatient gesture. "You sound like you're bargaining with me!"

She flushed and then said quite bravely, "That's what it is, isn't it? A bargain. All I'm asking is how long I have before you decide I'm not worth the wait."

His large hands clenched tightly around the fork, so tightly Chandra could see the whites of his knuckles, but his tone was low and steady. "Don't think," he advised, "that you can stall me indefinitely. I'm trying to be reasonable about this. . . ."

Chandra started to protest and then gave up. How could she make him see it was hardly a matter of reason? They were talking about a relationship in which she'd already lost her heart. She was madly, passionately in love with a man who thought in terms of mistresses and a domineering protectiveness, not in terms of love.

"Thank you, Reid," she finally managed, concentrating determinedly on her salad.

He looked up sharply. "Don't thank me," he muttered. "It's not as if I had much choice!"

She took a deep breath, trying to find a way back to more neutral territory. "I . . . I can at least thank you for what you did for me today," she went on steadily. "I'm very grateful, Reid, even if I didn't get to take the body count in person!"

"I'd rather not discuss it any further, if you don't mind," he stated coolly.

She bit her lip. "Whatever you like."

"Oh, Chandra, honey, I'm sorry for snapping at you," he groaned, setting down his fork. "I guess I'm a little on edge tonight."

"You never struck me as the nervous type," she managed to tease lightly, lifting her eyes to meet his with a smiling warmth.

"Normally, I'm not," he growled. "But around you . . ."

"Yes?" she prompted interestedly.

"Never mind. Eat your dinner and we'll take a walk around the marina. I need to work off some of the day's, uh, excitement!"

They did walk after dinner, lazily touring the elegant boats docked around the marina complex and enjoying the balmy evening air. Palm trees swayed luxuriantly overhead and herds of roller-skaters came and went in laughing, noisy clusters. Dodging roller-skaters was automatic for the slower-moving pedestrians.

When Reid eventually suggested he take her home, Chandra thought there was a curious reluctance in his voice, which confused her. Wasn't he looking forward to making love to her again tonight? She had been living with the knowledge that such a termination to the evening was inevitable and it had kept an almost constant ripple of excitement dancing through her bloodstream during the hectic day.

It hadn't occurred to her she could possibly refuse his advances. She thought herself amazingly lucky to have achieved the minor victory of not moving in with him. But the really genuine shock of the day came when Reid took her in his arms on her doorstep and made no move to come inside.

"Good night, honey," he said softly, gathering her close against him just before crushing her mouth under his. For an instant she was aware of all the hardness in him, the taut thighs, the muscles of his chest and shoulders, the heat of his body. Her bruised mouth absorbed the impact of his without protest, coming alive immediately as memories of the previous night sprang into instant awareness.

She was in the process of circling his neck with her arms when Reid abruptly stepped back. With a wry smile he captured her wrists in his strong hands and lowered them gently.

"I'll see you tomorrow after work, sweetheart." He stood looking at her with that familiar hunger blazing in the glacial depths of his eyes. But he only stood there for a moment and then he was gone. A few seconds later the black Ferrari purred off into the night.

The rest of the week, much to Chandra's gathering dismay, proceeded in much the same nerve-racking manner. Reid dutifully met her after work and took her out to dinner or ate a meal she had prepared. They spent the evening together talking of everything from California's zany politics to the proper way to make a Caesar salad. Once Reid took her dancing.

But regardless of how they spent the time, each evening concluded in exactly the same fashion. Reid would leave her on her doorstep with a quick, hard kiss and then stride briskly away to climb into the Ferrari.

Chandra was going nuts by Friday and she knew it. Friday afternoon she stood at the window of her office, staring at passing roller-skaters and young men carrying surfboards without really seeing either.

What was going wrong? She was getting frightened and she knew it. Something wasn't right and she didn't know how to force the issue. How did you say to a man, Why aren't you sleeping with me? Especially after you'd told that man you wouldn't move in with him.

She bit her lip and took a grip on her nerves. Reid couldn't possibly have believed anything Blaine had told him that night in Coronado, could he? Would it have mattered if he did? What lies might Sherwood have fed him to make Reid think twice about the kind of association he wanted with Chandra?

He'd promised her his protection and he was a blatantly honest man. Would he feel obliged to stick by his promise even though he no longer wanted her as a mistress?

The thought sent a cold frisson along her spine. What if Reid didn't want her any longer and was trying to find a polite way out of the relationship?

She was chewing her lower lip into a painful fullness when the phone rang.

"Line one, Chandra," Alicia called out cheerfully, unaware of her boss's growing discomfort.

Reluctantly Chandra lifted the receiver.

"Chandra?" Reid's voice came clear and strong. "Just wanted to let you know I'm going to be tied up with that client who wants the additions to his shopping center. Don't wait dinner for me, honey," he finished casually. "I'll call you when I'm through here."

"All right, Reid," she whispered, a horrible feeling of genuine despair creeping over her. She felt exactly like the wife who learns her husband is "working late at the office."

Dismally she hung up the phone and sank bleakly into her chair. What was going on? She certainly had no right to behave like a jealous wife and she had as little right to behave like a jealous lover. Hell, she thought disgustedly, slinging a pencil across the desktop, she didn't even have any right to behave like a jealous mistress!

What role was she playing in Reid's life now? Confused and angry, Chandra tried to reason out his actions, but the more she thought about it the more confused and angry she grew. It was probably inevitable that when the phone rang once more shortly before five, she was in a mood to seek a temporary escape from her problems.

"Chandra, old pal," sang out the familiar voice of Carol Simpson, a casual friend with whom she occasionally went shopping or had lunch. "The gang is going down to the

121

usual place after work'and someone noticed we haven't seen you in a while. Join us?"

Chandra jumped at the opportunity. "I'd love to," she said quickly, thinking that any way of passing the next few hours was preferable to cooling her heels at home waiting for a call that might be very late in coming.

Once the decision had been made, Chandra didn't hesitate. She gathered her leather bag and car keys, said good night to Alicia, who was on her way out the door, and then paused, her hand on the light switch.

For a second she stood staring at the telephone and then she walked back across the room to dial Reid's number. His secretary answered and offered at once to put her through.

"That's all right," Chandra said quickly, "I only wanted to give him a message. Perhaps you could leave it for him so that he'll see it when he's through with his client?"

"No problem," the woman said cheerfully.

Chandra rattled off the name of the popular after-work lounge where she was going. "Tell him I'll be there until about seven. I'll call him at home when I'm through." That had a nice sound to it, she decided with satisfaction as she replaced the receiver. *She'd* call *him!* There was a certain pleasing air of taking charge in the line. It was nice to reverse the roles. From the beginning of the relationship, it seemed to be Reid who had taken charge.

The popular restaurant lounge was vibrantly alive with the young professional crowd that patronized it as an after-work spot. The restaurant, aware of the profit that flowed so nicely from the energetic, fast-living, well-salaried group, provided a lavish buffet of Mexican delicacies and thus encouraged a repeat business. Margaritas were sold at half price by the pitcher and the general atmosphere was one of cheerful, slick pleasure-seeking.

"Chandra! Over here!"

In the dimly lit surroundings Chandra picked out her

friend Carol and the rest of the familiar group. Within minutes she was absorbed into the crowd.

Someone poured her a margarita from the pitcher and Chandra sipped it very tentatively. It was probably her destiny to be reminded of that first morning in Reid's bed whenever she drank the tequila and lime juice mixture. She had a momentary vision of herself at the age of ninety-five, drinking margaritas and wondering why she hadn't had the sense to move in with Reid without making such a fuss. Under her friends' laughing influence, she thrust the image aside. She needed a little of the superficial cheer emanating from her group of acquaintances, she told herself.

Idly she listened to talk of wind-surfing, sailing, a comparison of gyms and racquetball courts, and the various other topics that were of such earthshaking interest locally. Already the pairs were beginning to form around the table, she thought with sardonic objectivity. In such a young, attractive crowd, few would find themselves alone on Saturday morning.

She was a part of this group and yet not a part of it, she realized dimly. She hadn't been one of the casual lovers who floated in and out of each other's arms so freely. Except, of course, she reminded herself with a wince, for the morning she'd awakened in Reid's bed!

"You look," said an unfamiliar voice at her elbow, "as if you could use a bit of cheering up!"

Chandra turned her head to smile automatically at the good-looking, sandy-haired young man with the perfectly trimmed mustache as he sank languidly down onto the seat beside her.

"Sorry," she said brightly, "it's been a long week."

"Don't I know it!" he groaned good-naturedly, leaning back in his chair with a casual sprawl that allowed an intimate glimpse of his chest. The gold chains around his neck and the shirt unbuttoned halfway to his stomach went with the appropriately faded jeans.

"Are you new in the group?" Chandra asked politely, for something to say. He didn't look nearly as good in his jeans as Reid did. He looked a little soft, a bit foppish, despite the casual attire. But, then, Reid would have looked all virile male regardless of what he wore!

"I'm a friend of Pete's." He indicated a dark-haired young man across the table who was attentively bent over the blonde beside him. "Name's Jerry." He poured her another margarita and smiled invitingly.

"I'm Chandra," she said politely. Last names weren't needed.

For several minutes she managed the necessary casual chatter, deliberately ignoring the sexual innuendoes and invitations lying under the surface. Jerry wasn't making any secret of his ultimate purpose, although there were a great many comments about the importance of two people coming together and sharing some space. Chandra saw through him so easily she had to hide a smile on occasion. It wouldn't be long before Jerry got the hint and looked elsewhere for the meaningful relationship that might last all weekend.

But she must have been doing a better job of holding up her end of the conversation than she realized, because a few minutes later Jerry smiled at her with open invitation.

"Have dinner with me tonight? I know a place where we can get the best lobster in town!"

Chandra blinked, not fully realizing how she had let things progress quite this far. To give her something to do while she made up her mind how to handle the situation, she picked up the salt-rimmed margarita glass and was on the point of taking a hasty sip when a large, tanned hand reached down over her left shoulder and deftly removed the birdbath-shaped glass from her fingers.

For an instant Chandra stared in shock at the hand. She'd have recognized it anywhere. The faint sprinkling of copper hair on the back and the square, strong fingers were arrestingly familiar.

124

The margarita glass was set back down on the table and Chandra kept staring at it, feeling a little stricken. She could sense the unpleasant vibrations emanating from Reid even before he spoke.

"If I'd known," he drawled in that sandpapery voice, "that you wanted to relive last weekend, I'd have arranged to make up a batch of my own special margarita recipe. You remember how much you liked it, honey?"

But there was nothing particularly warm and affectionate about the endearment. Slowly Chandra lifted her wary hazel eyes to meet his gaze. It struck her very forcibly that she'd never seen the glaciers looking quite so cold.

"Hello, Reid," she forced herself to say with cheerful calm. "I see you got my message."

"I did. I decided not to wait for your call," he added with silky menace as he towered beside her chair.

"So I see. Well, as long as you're here," she went on gamely, aware of Jerry's uneasy reaction to the small scene, "why don't you sit down and have a drink? I'll introduce you . . ."

The bleak landscape of his face was a fitting backdrop for the freezing cold in those blue and gray eyes, she thought wretchedly as she continued to search his features for some hint of softening. What right did he have to be so upset about a minor thing like this?

"No, thanks," he said with an angry brusqueness. He clamped his hand around her wrist and hauled her effortlessly to her feet. "Say good night to your friend," he instructed with barely concealed fierceness.

"Good night, Jerry," she managed obediently, twisting her hand uselessly in its manacle.

Jerry shrugged and turned away, his eyes on a cute redhead at the end of the table. The evening was getting on. He had to line up something fairly soon or risk the ignominy of spending the weekend alone.

"Not very nice of you to make him waste so much

125

time," Reid growled softly as he yanked her toward the door.

"We were talking! Just because you consider it a waste of time to talk to a woman unless you're going to go to bed with her doesn't mean every man does!" They were the first words that came to mind and they were apparently among the worst she could have chosen.

"You've got a hell of a lot of nerve making accusations like that," he snarled as he located the Ferrari in the parking lot and shoved her inside. "Haven't you been paying attention at all during the past few days? I've been doing a lot of talking, in case you hadn't noticed, and not asking for much in return except a good-night kiss!"

"Reid! My car!" Chandra twisted in her seat to search out the battered Porsche carefully parked some distance from any other car.

"No one's going to steal that poor thing. Don't worry about it, you can get it in the morning! You've got other things to occupy your thoughts tonight!"

"Such as?" she got out tightly. "I suppose I could get fairly involved in a tirade about your rude manners and your lack of any right to drag me out of that lounge! But I'd probably be going through the exercise for nothing. Something tells me you don't respond to well-meant criticism!"

"Perhaps not, but I do respond very quickly to messages telling me my woman is out enjoying herself at a popular singles bar simply because I had a business engagement and was going to be a little late!" he shot back bitterly, guiding the Ferrari out of the parking lot and turning toward La Jolla.

"Well, at least you do respond to something!" she shot back gamely, determined not to be outdone when it came to accusations. She was aware of the barely repressed violence in him but nothing could have enforced caution on her in that moment. The anger and frustration and uncertainty of the past week were spilling over in a huge

126

wave. Besides, she admitted very privately, she was reasonably safe as long as he had his hands full fighting Friday evening traffic!

"What the devil do you mean by that crack?" he snapped, flinging her a scathing glance.

"I mean that for the past week you haven't seemed particularly interested in responding to your . . . your *mistress!*" It was very hard to say the word for some reason.

"Is that why you took the first opportunity to go racing off and find another lover? Because you thought I wasn't interested in you any longer?" The sheer disbelief fairly thundered in his voice. "Why, you crazy, idiotic female! I ought to take a belt to your backside!"

"Do you deny it?" she blazed righteously, glaring at his harshly set profile. She saw his hands tighten on the wheel. "You haven't asked anything more than a good-night kiss of me for days!"

"Oh, my God!" he breathed, looking appalled. "I can't believe this!"

"And furthermore," she roared on, unstoppable now, "I wasn't looking for a . . . a lover in that bar. I was invited to join some friends after work and, since you were *busy,* I felt free to do so! What's wrong with that?"

"You know damn well why people go to places like that lounge!"

"They go there to mingle with friends!"

"They go there to find someone. to spend the night with!"

"That wasn't the reason I went!" she yelled across the leather seat. "But even if it was, what difference would it make to you?" They were in La Jolla and presently they would be pulling into Reid's drive. She ought to be toning down the argument but Chandra didn't think she was capable of it at that moment.

"I'll tell you what difference it makes to me, you little fool! I happen to expect my woman to stay loyal to me.

I know that might strike you as an outmoded way of thinking in this day and age and especially here in southern California, but it's the way I am!" He slammed the car to a halt in the drive and threw open the door.

Chandra was out of her side before he could circle the hood. Hastily she backed away as he started toward her. He really was furious, she thought unhappily. But that didn't give him any right to treat her like this!

"Reid, listen to me," she began very firmly. But the effect of her attempt at dignity was totally wiped out by her steady retreat. She was backing through the serene Japanese-style garden that wrapped the house. As with many such gardens it was designed with a focus, and the stone paths channeled a visitor toward the far end. With quick glances over her shoulder, Chandra kept edging toward the lush grottolike arrangement behind her.

"That's been my mistake this past week," he alleged, pacing her deliberately with lean, hungry strides. "I tried listening to you. I tried to give you some time. I *tried,*" he emphasized vengefully, "to make you see me as your knight in shining armor!"

"What?" she shrieked, absolutely astonished.

"I know," he grated, "I was a fool. Believe me, it won't happen again. You've made it very clear you don't really want a self-denying knight after all. You want a man who *responds* to you!"

"Reid, wait a minute!" Chandra pleaded, almost upon the grotto and terribly aware there was no way back out of the garden except past him. She'd been a fool to start her retreat in this direction. Perhaps that's why he hadn't rushed her yet. He knew she was working toward a dead end.

"I had no idea you were trying to be . . . to be chivalrous," she explained helplessly, spreading her fingers wide in a placating gesture that did nothing to halt him. Her foot sought for purchase on the first of the tiny steps leading up to the fern and rock-guarded grotto. Automatically she glanced down to make certain of her footing.

"If that's what they call going home to a cold shower every night, then that's what I was trying to be!" he told her grittily. "I can't thank you enough for setting me straight. God only knows how much longer I might have hung on trying to earn a little appreciation of my better nature!"

"But I didn't understand!" she squeaked, feeling as if she were being made to walk a plank as she shakily gained another step. She could hear the water in the fountain pool behind her, splashing merrily. "I thought Blaine had told you something so awful about me you no longer felt the same . . ."

"How many times have I told you I could care less about your past?" he charged, his foot on the bottom step, as he turned accusing eyes on her. "As it happens, Sherwood didn't tell me anything at all about you. I did all the talking that day!"

"Oh, Reid," she breathed, "I'm so glad! I . . . I thought . . ."

"You're not getting out of this with the flimsy little excuse that you didn't properly comprehend my motives!" he menaced, taking the next step. "When I think of the way I've suffered for the past few nights . . ."

She read the grim intent in his face and panicked. He wasn't anywhere near over his anger and he was reaching for her . . .

Chandra turned, making an attempt to edge along the narrow, rocky rim of the bubbling pool and, in her anxious haste, predictably enough, lost her footing.

She had time to realize it wasn't a decorative fountain she was falling into with such appalling lack of grace, but a concealed hot tub. In the next instant she plunged into the frothy hot water.

CHAPTER EIGHT

"Damn you, Reid Devlin!"

The cry was a sputtering, choking speech of pure feminine rage as Chandra floundered to her feet in the hot surging water. She stood breast-high in the tub, her hair hanging in streaming tendrils around her face, clothes plastered to her body. Furiously she glared at him, hazel eyes almost green with the force of her emotions.

He stood on the edge of the rockery that concealed the redwood hot tub, towering over her in the rapidly falling dusk of the summer night.

"Don't blame me for your natural clumsiness!" he retorted, eyes gleaming with malicious satisfaction and something else, something Chandra didn't trust at all.

"Why not?" she charged angrily. "It's your fault I fell in! If you hadn't *driven* me back into the garden I would never have . . ."

"Driven you!" he repeated incredulously, his hands forming fists on his lean hips as his eyes raked her wet, infuriated features and then went lower to settle on the thrust of nipples against clinging fabric. "I didn't drive you into that tub, you walked right in of your own free will! But regardless of how you got there," he went on grimly, "you deserved it. You deserve a hell of a lot more than that, in fact!"

"I've already apologized for my slight misunderstanding of your behavior this past week," Chandra bit out scathingly, sinking to her chin in the water in order to prevent his aggressive, masculine stare from centering on her breasts. She found herself rebelling against the possessive flare in the glacial gaze. He had no right to look at her like that after the way he'd acted.

"You think a mealymouthed apology is going to make up for what I've been through?" he flung back, face granite-hard.

"Come on now, Reid," she snapped waspishly. "A few cold showers can't have been all that bad!"

"I'm not just talking about the wasted nights this past week, I'm talking about what you put me through tonight when you went scampering off to flirt at that singles bar!"

"I was not flirting! It was an after-work drink with some friends of mine. People do it all the time!" she nearly shouted.

"People go there to find a weekend roommate and you know it!" he declared righteously.

"If you know so much about it, you must have been the route a few times yourself!"

"Don't try to bring my behavior into this discussion," he rapped. "It's you we're raking over the coals!"

"Well, I don't see what gives you the right," she tossed back rashly, feeling very much at a disadvantage trying to defend herself when she was up to her neck, quite literally, in hot water. Her stern accuser stood on the edge of the pool and stared at her as if she'd taken leave of her senses.

"You don't see what gives me the right!" he snarled, as if astounded by some new evidence of stupidity. "My God, woman, what does it take? Didn't you learn anything at all about rights that night you accepted my protection? I thought I made things perfectly clear while you were in my bed. But apparently you became confused by my actions during the past few days. Believe me, I won't allow you any more room for leaping to false conclusions!"

"Reid! What are you doing?" Chandra yelped, backing to the wall of the tub as he kicked off his shoes and vaulted over the edge into the hot water. "Your clothes!" It was the only protest she could come up with in that alarming moment.

He waded toward her through the surging warmth, looking for all the world like some implacable primitive male out to subdue a recalcitrant woman.

"Don't worry about my clothes," he gibed, reaching for her as she vainly tried to scramble out of reach. "I won't be needing them in a minute, anyway!"

"If you think I'm going to let you manhandle me . . . !" she began, outraged and trying desperately to slip out of the grip he had on her blouse.

"That isn't quite the word I would have picked, but maybe it's accurate enough at that!"

Reid's fingers tightened warningly on the handful of wet material he'd managed to grasp as Chandra struggled determinedly. When she made a lunge toward the side of the pool where the steps led to the surface there was a sudden release of restraint and she knew the blouse had torn under the water.

An instant later, he'd pulled it free completely, discarding the fabric in favor of caging her against the circular wall. Naked from the waist up, Chandra once again sank to the level of her chin, knowing her body was heating under the impact of the enforced intimacy. Once again the gray-blue depths of his gaze sought her curving breasts, which were alternately revealed and then concealed by the foaming water.

"Did you really think," he rasped deeply, his strong, square hands firmly planted on either side of her shoulders, his body pressing close to hers, "that I'd let you get away with flitting off to that lounge this evening?"

"I didn't think it mattered all that much!" she declared stonily, her eyes focusing on the wet fabric of the shirt covering his chest. She suddenly discovered it was too dangerous to meet his eyes. "Besides," she ploughed on bravely, "you know I'd never have gone off with anyone there!"

A short paused followed that remark, a pause that succeeded in forcing her eyes back up to his face. He was
watching her with a curious mixture of irritation and
desire. She knew his body was reacting to her naked helplessness in the water.

"I know," he agreed almost harshly. "So why did you
go?"

"I told you!" she stormed wretchedly, relieved on the
one hand that he really did believe she had no disloyal
intentions and annoyed on the other that he was taking
her to task over the matter.

"I heard something about thinking I might not be interested in you any longer," he drawled, letting his jean-clad
hips glide tantalizingly against hers for an instant. "And
I hear talk of rights. . . . But what was the real reason,
Chandra? Any chance you were deliberately trying to
make me jealous? Did you decide to find out what I'd do
if I thought you were flirting with someone else?"

She heard the scratch of the sandpaper against the velvet and shivered in the hot water. Bravely she met his eyes.
Had that been in the back of her mind when she'd accepted the invitation to join the gang for a drink? Had she been
subconsciously wondering if Reid would come after her?
No, that was childish! She wouldn't have done a thing like
that!

"Of course not!" she defended briskly, feeling foolish
with her hands covering her breasts under the water. But
she couldn't hold that clashing gaze for long and as soon
as she said the words she went back to staring at the
straining wet buttons on his chest.

"Chandra?" The sandpaper was almost gone now, the
thick velvet heavy and inviting as he lowered his head to
drop the tiniest, most intriguing of kisses just under her
earlobe.

"Wh-what?" she managed, drawing in a deep, steadying
breath at the dangerous little caress.

"Tell me the truth, little, one," he urged. There came

133

another of the intriguing miniature kisses, this time under the other earlobe.

"Oh, Reid," she breathed, succumbing to the coaxing, gentling approach almost immediately. She squeezed her eyes shut as his fingertips tracked lightly down her arms and his hands closed over hers as she still tried to cover her breasts. "I . . . I think maybe I was trying to see if you'd come after me. I didn't understand your actions this week. I was terrified you didn't want me any longer, that you were only sticking around because you felt you'd made some sort of bargain you had to uphold . . ."

"Chandra." Her name was an infinitely soft, infinitely appealing sound as he gently pulled her protective hands away from the curving fullness they'd been hiding. As his fingers replaced hers, gliding over the tautening nipples, she sighed in a kind of relieved surrender. He did want her.

"How could you doubt me, sweetheart?" he muttered thickly.

"I don't know, Reid," she whispered, her hands going to his waist as he continued to caress her lightly under the water. Eyes still closed, she leaned her head against his shoulder. "I suppose I'm just not used to our relationship yet."

"I see," he stated evenly. "Well, let me make one point very clear about our 'relationship.'" A new inflection in his words alerted her, and Chandra lifted her head with a touch of wariness to meet the diamond coldness in his eyes.

"If you," he went on very distinctly, all velvet gone from his voice, "ever try a stunt like that again, I promise you I'll retaliate in such a basic, elementary, straightforward fashion that even you won't be able to misinterpret my actions!"

"Are you threatening to beat me?" she blazed, incensed as she realized his momentary softening had been a ruse to get her to admit the truth. She released her hold on his waist and planted her hands on his shoulders, pushing fruitlessly.

"You'd better believe it," he retorted immediately, his hands circling her ribs to lock behind her back. Effortlessly he pulled her against his wet, still-clad body, his face very close to her mutinous one.

"Then you can damn well unthreaten me! I don't respond to that sort of approach!"

"No?" he mocked, burying his face in her throat with sudden, undisguised passion. "Then how about this one?"

"Reid!" she gasped, aware of his hands going to the snap of her jeans and prying it open. "Wait, please! I must know!"

"Know what?" he murmured, his hands slipping inside her jeans to ease them down over her hips.

"I want to know why you were trying to play Don Quixote this past week!" she begged, struggling to halt his hands.

"Damned if I know," he admitted disinterestedly. "I guess I went crazy."

"That's not a good enough reason!"

"Why not? It's the reason every self-respecting southern Californian uses to explain the inexplicable."

The inexplicable. Dazedly Chandra shook her head in mute denial, but it was too late to insist on a better explanation. He had almost completed the task of stripping her wet jeans from her body, and a moment later he lifted her weightlessly in one arm to conclude the effort. The soaking denim was tossed negligently onto the edge of the tub as he continued to cradle her in one arm.

"So you didn't think I was interested in you any longer, you foolish woman," he breathed hoarsely, his eyes sweeping the nearly nude length of her as she lay half-submerged against him.

The blue and gray gaze halted momentarily on the scrap of underwear still clinging to her hips and then he casually ripped it free, heedless of the ruined fabric.

"I'll show you how much I want you," he vowed, releasing her to struggle with his own wet clothes.

"If you think I'm going to let you make love to me after the way you just blew up, you really are crazy!" she informed him challengingly. Provoked by his easy assumption of possessive right even though her body was reacting fiercely to the hunger and intent in his face, she tried to maintain some control. They had a great deal to discuss, she decided resolutely, such as why he had elected to try and imitate his version of a chivalrous protector all week!

"Come here," he commanded with soft, velvety roughness. "Come here and find out what happens when you decide to play games with a man who wants you as badly as I do!"

She shivered beneath the implied touch and deliberately took another sliding step out of reach. There was a new element in the heated atmosphere. She sensed it and responded to it on one level even while she continued to resist the coaxing order. It was a primitive, savage little skirmish between a man and a woman with both knowing and wanting the final outcome. What was it that sometimes drove the female of the species to make life difficult for the male? Chandra wondered as she continued to edge away, barely beyond Reid's touch.

There was a marvelous, exhilarating sense of freedom as she floated and glided naked in the deliciously warm water. Chandra felt her sense of danger heighten as Reid's eyes narrowed in warning.

"You can't escape, you know," Reid murmured with lazy menace. She saw the flickering desire in his eyes as he slowly moved to close the distance between them.

"No?" she taunted lightly, thrillingly aware of the advancing strength in him. The tub wasn't very large, being expressly designed for intimate bathing. They both knew he could reach out and take her any time he wished.

"Definitely not. You have far too much to pay for tonight, my sweet. A man has to put his foot down at some point or risk having his woman get completely out of hand."

"You sound very knowledgeable on the subject," she noted coolly.

"I figure I'm in the same position as that peacock we saw at the zoo the other day," Reid agreed willingly. "I've spent nearly a week displaying my beautiful feathers and you show your appreciation by calmly going off to drink another man's margaritas."

She sighed ruefully, her hands sweeping back and forth under the surface of the bubbling water. "I thought I'd explained about that," she murmured.

"You did. That doesn't mean you're going to get off scot-free!" he said quietly. "Besides, I've learned my lesson. I'm going to stop wasting valuable time displaying unappreciated plumage!"

With a sudden, swooping action, he had her once again in his arms, drawing her naked body close and tangling her legs with his.

Helpless against his chest, Chandra braced her fingers on his shoulders and gazed up longingly into his face. For an instant they simply stared at each other, letting the heat of their mutual passion show in their eyes.

And then Reid took the open invitation of her lips, his mouth closing over hers in compelling mastery and need.

Chandra's hands moved to bury themselves in the coppery dampness of his hair as she arched into his hard leanness. As soon as his mouth had touched hers, the small display of resistance evaporated from her body. She loved this man and she knew it would always be like this whenever he touched her.

"I don't think I could have lasted much longer in the role of Sir Lancelot, anyway," Reid rasped against her lips.

"Oh, I don't know," she teased breathlessly as his hands slipped down her naked spine to press her hips tightly against him. "You were doing awfully well there for a while!"

"A facade that undoubtedly would have crumpled completely this evening, regardless of the provocation you insisted on providing!"

He was supporting her weight full against him now, her toes not even touching the bottom of the tub. She felt the scrape of copper hair against the slick, wet skin of her breasts and trembled.

"Oh, Reid, my darling, Reid," she whispered as his lips moved to the nape of her neck and then to the pulse of her throat.

She felt herself lifted higher out of the water as strong hands clamped around her narrow waist. He bent his head to kiss first one breast and then the other, curling his tongue around the hardening nipples in a passionate caress that made her cry out softly.

She ran her hands down the length of his ribs, gently raking his flanks with her nails, and gloried in the response she elicited.

"I've spent almost a week trying to sleep at night with memories of how you'd been in my bed," he muttered. He was stepping backward, pulling her with him through the water, and she realized he was heading for the tub steps. But he didn't try to climb them. Instead he lowered himself to the underwater bench and settled her across his lap, only her head and shoulders above the surface.

His hand moved over her body, exploring, remembering, urging, and Chandra sagged against him, thrust her fingertips through the wet hair of his chest. With mesmerized wonder she followed the tapering shape of his body, seeking the hardness of his thighs and the tensed muscles of his stomach.

"You've got to stay with me, honey. You've got to live with me. I don't have the patience to woo you any longer . . ."

"Woo me!" she repeated thickly, her eyes wide and

loving. "Is that what you were trying to do this past week? Woo me into coming and living with you?"

"I guess so," he admitted, as if his motives hadn't been entirely clear, even to himself. "All I know is that I was trying to attract you, trying to make you want me enough to agree to live with me. I need you in my life, Chandra, not as someone to date when I feel like it, but as a part of my everyday living. I want you in my bed and my shower and seated across the table from me at dinner. Can't you give me that much, sweetheart? I'll take care of you—haven't I already proven that?"

"Yes," she whispered huskily, knowing she couldn't deny him what he asked. "You've already proven that. And if it means so much to you, I will come and live with you."

He looked down into her glowing, promising eyes and suddenly it became very hard to draw a deep breath under the forcefulness of his hungering, savagely satisfied expression. In other circumstances, she told herself fleetingly as he fastened his mouth passionately on hers, she might have been accepting a man's proposal of marriage. With Reid there would be no marriage, but she knew the strength of his emotions went deeper than those of many men who might have offered a ring. She would be satisfied with that much, she swore.

"You won't regret it, Chandra, I promise you won't regret it!"

The hand moving on her body became fiercely urgent, sending a clamoring summons to her senses as Chandra's mind began to whirl in delighted surrender. There had never been a man in her life who could make her feel like this. Surely it wasn't so wrong to accept him on his terms?

Then she put the wistful thoughts out of her head entirely as he moved her, resettling her body on top of his so that she was lying along his outstretched length.

"Reid?" she questioned uncertainly, aware that in her

139

passion she was more than willing to comply with his wishes but not quite sure what it was he intended.

He gazed down at her as she rested her chin against his chest, his eyes full of passionate humor. "Don't you know the real reason hot tubs became so popular out here on the West Coast?"

"Reid!" she squeaked, startled. "In the *water?*"

"Why not?" he grinned wickedly, pulling her hips firmly down onto his and anchoring her idling legs with his ankles.

"We'll drown!" she offered in laughing objection.

"Trust me," he urged thickly, his hands pressing her weightless body against him.

"I do," she breathed in abrupt and total sincerity. "Oh, Reid, I trust you completely!"

The grin disappeared from his face as he accepted her words and the total honesty in her eyes. Could he see the love that was there? she wondered. He wouldn't want that, she knew. She hoped he read it only as trust and passion and didn't see the underlying support of a love unlike anything else she had ever felt. But how could he see it? He didn't believe in such an emotion in the first place!

"My own, sweet Chandra," he murmured, and then his body was surging against hers as he held her firmly in place.

The heavy rhythm was slowed and somehow intensified by the slight resistance offered by the water. It created an incredibly languid, erotically graceful sensation that at once tantalized and thrilled.

Slowly at first and then with increasing urgency Chandra caught the pattern of the movement. Her body responded as it always would to Reid's power, adapting to the aquatic environment of his lovemaking with a willingness that bespoke her own passion.

"My God, Chandra!" he gasped, his hands clenched tightly into her hips as he guided the lovemaking. "You drive me crazy, woman!"

140

Those were the last coherent words either of them spoke as the sounds from their throats became as primordial and timeless as the watery surroundings. After what seemed an endless exploration of the sea of their passion the liquid around them seemed to churn faster and faster. Chandra felt as if it had suddenly become a plunging river heading for the headlong cascade of a waterfall somewhere up ahead.

Deliriously she gave herself over to the rush, aware only of the support of Reid's arms and the raging strength of his body as he went over the falls with her.

Somehow Reid managed to keep both their heads above water as they lay quiescent for a long time in the churning froth. Content in her love, Chandra left the problem of not going under to him. She could trust Reid. He would always take care of her. She felt his fingers stroking back her wet hair and nestled happily against his chest.

"I thought you were afraid of drowning," he teased affectionately, indicating her complete lack of interest in supporting herself out of the water.

"I think I already did. Too late to worry about it now," she explained blissfully.

He laughed, a sound she felt deep in the broad chest beneath her.

"I'm the one who's in too deep," he complained softly. "I've known it from the beginning . . ."

But the soft wonder of the moment was abruptly shattered by the sound of a car's engine in the drive, and whatever else Reid might have said was lost.

"Damn," he growled ferociously, setting her gently on her feet in the water. "Of all the times to have visitors."

"Our clothes!" Chandra glanced helplessly at the soggy garments strewn along the edge of the tub and floating in the foam.

"I keep a couple of towels stored in that little chest over there," he said, scrambling with enviable grace out of the pool and striding across the stones to a decorative stand

141

behind a clump of ferns. Bending down he pulled out two large white towels, wrapped one around his waist, and held another open invitingly.

"Out you get," he ordered briskly. "You can dry off and then go into the house via the back way while I deal with whoever's out front."

"But I don't have anything dry to put on!" she protested, climbing carefully out of the hot water and stepping gratefully into the thick towel.

"You can hunt through my closet. You should be able to find something. Don't worry, I'll get rid of our visitor!"

"Will you, Reid? I'm not sure I want to be got rid of!"

Chandra whirled at the sultry feminine voice, whipping the white towel around her body with a frantic movement.

"So you still have the hot tub, I see, darling. And you're putting it to good use, too, or should I say you're putting it to the use I would have expected of you?"

She was beautiful, Chandra thought bleakly. A stunning redhead with blue-green eyes and a well-displayed, voluptuous figure. She was probably a couple of years older than Chandra at the most, but that may have been a misleading impression. There was a look of worldly experience about the woman that made it difficult to judge her age. She was cool and poised, while Chandra felt like an idiot, dripping in her towel.

The other woman was wearing a silk blouse unbuttoned well below her breasts and a pair of white shorts cut high on the leg. Brilliant scarlet fingernails tipped her hands and a well-defined mouth was done in a matching shade. The mass of windswept red hair was anchored by a stylish turquoise band that matched the blouse. Long, shapely legs ended in tiny, strappy sandals. The woman didn't look as if she'd accidentally tripped or stumbled into a pool in her life. She looked quite California-perfect.

Reid moved before he spoke, putting himself between Chandra and the newcomer. Chandra was grateful for the protectiveness of the action but she still felt horribly ridiculous in the towel.

"Hello, Marilyn," he said in a calm, stony voice that would have sent Chandra packing if she'd been standing in Marilyn's little strappy sandals but that didn't seem to faze the other woman in the least.

"Hello, darling. It's been a long time." The blue-green eyes swept over Reid assessingly as if he were a prize stud animal.

"Not nearly long enough," he assured her feelingly. "What do you want?"

"To talk," the woman shrugged, flicking a hard glance at Chandra, who was standing very still behind Reid's shoulder. "Alone."

"Alone?" Although Chandra couldn't see his expression she knew one dark brow was arching in quelling rebuke. "I'm afraid that's not necessary," he went on coldly. "Whatever you have to say can be said in front of Chandra."

"You want your current girl friend listening in on a private discussion between us, Reid?" the beautiful Marilyn taunted easily. "Don't you think that might embarrass her?"

"Why should it?" Reid asked in a hard voice. "Chandra's more than a girl friend. She's the most important woman in my life. In fact," he went on with heavy emphasis, "she's the only woman in my life!"

"For the moment," Marilyn chuckled throatily, turning her gaze back to Chandra. "Since he's not going to do the proper thing and introduce us, it looks like we'll have to manage on our own. I'm Marilyn Hastings, Reid's ex-wife."

Chandra opened her mouth to try to make some kind of acknowledgment to the introduction only to be silenced by Reid speaking first.

"This is Chandra Madison," he said swiftly. "My fiancée."

It was hard to say, Chandra decided later, which of the two women was the most thoroughly surprised. But in the end she knew she had the advantage over Marilyn Hastings.

Because in the few shocked seconds it took her to recover from being introduced as Reid's future wife, Chandra realized what he was doing.

Once again Reid had extended his protection to her. He had moved to protect her from the malice in the other woman by giving Chandra an unassailable position.

CHAPTER NINE

"Reid, you go out and talk to her," Chandra hissed in a low voice a few minutes later as she pulled on a toweling robe and belted it around her waist. It fell almost to her knees and certainly provided enough modesty but Chandra still felt undressed. "Whatever she wants to say is between the two of you. It doesn't concern me."

On the other side of the bedroom Reid finished clasping a wide belt around his waist and reached for a shirt. He slanted a long glance at her and shook his head once.

"No. You heard me tell her I'm going to marry you. She won't believe that if you cower in the bedroom!"

Chandra's face softened as she came toward him around the wide bed.

"I know why you said what you did," she smiled, "and I'm very grateful. You really are determined to protect me, aren't you? But you must see it's a little awkward . . ."

He watched her earnest face for a moment and then said calmly, "I want you with me."

Chandra drew a deep breath. Was this the price she was expected to pay for her latest "protection"? A confrontation with an ex-wife? But there was no arguing with Reid in his present mood. He had that determined, absolutely implacable expression etched into his hard features.

"All right, Reid. If you're sure . . ."

"I'm sure." There was no velvet now in his voice.

He took her arm and walked her through the white and

chrome bedroom, down the skylit hall, and out into the dazzling white living room. Marilyn was curled into a corner of the white couch, a splash of color against the unending lightness around her. Chandra knew in an instant the pose was studied. It was also, she reflected wryly, effective.

"I am sorry to interrupt that little scene in the pool, Chandra dear," the redhead began with sultry mockery as she ran an eye over Chandra's straight wet hair and belted terry robe. "I hope you'll forgive me?"

"It's not important," Chandra said with false easiness. "Reid and I were on our way out, anyway."

"Have you and my ex-husband been engaged very long?" Marilyn went on chattily as if Reid wasn't in the room.

"No, not long."

"I didn't think so," Marilyn purred in satisfaction. "I see you're not wearing a ring."

"Chandra's ring is none of your business, Marilyn," Reid interposed wearily. "Suppose you just tell us the reason for this little visit. I thought you were happily finding yourself up in Los Angeles?"

"I was, darling, but when I heard about the new lady in your life, I decided to come down and see her for myself." She turned her head briefly to Chandra with a quick smile that didn't reach her blue-green eyes. "Sheer curiosity, I'm afraid, dear. One of the drawbacks to being an 'ex.' A woman always finds herself wondering what the new girl friend is like!"

"How did you hear about Chandra?" Reid interrupted roughly. He was sitting close to Chandra on a large white hassock but his steady gaze was on his ex-wife. He was watching her the way one would watch a deadly snake.

"It seems you gave a party last weekend, and one of the guests, who happens to be a mutual friend," Marilyn tossed in as an aside to Chandra, "noticed the rather close relationship that seemed to have developed between you, Reid, and your, uh, hired hostess for the evening."

The way she said "hired hostess" left no doubt in Chandra's mind that the word call girl could have been substituted. Quite suddenly she was even more grateful for the fake status of fiancée that Reid had given her on the spur of the moment. He must have known how his ex-wife's mind worked. Nevertheless, memories of her behavior that night made Chandra's face flush, and she knew Marilyn must have seen it.

"Now that your curiosity is satisfied and you've met my future wife perhaps you'll be good enough to leave?" Reid asked curtly.

"Aren't you even going to offer me a drink, darling? For old times' sake? You used to make the best margaritas in town. Have you ever sampled Reid's margaritas, Chandra?" Marilyn tossed her a bright, expectant glance.

From out of nowhere Chandra's sense of humor finally surged to the fore. She returned the mockingly bright smile with one of her own and said on a note of intimate laughter that she combined with a deliberate sidelong glance at Reid, "Funny you should mention Reid's margaritas, Marilyn!"

Reid caught her eye and the glacial eyes melted in momentary humor. There was no way Marilyn could have missed the implication of a very private joke, and when Chandra met the other woman's eyes once more, she saw the point had gone home.

"Well, then," the redhead began determinedly, as if seeking to recover lost ground, "are you going to offer me one?"

"I don't think so," Reid drawled calmly. "Chandra and I were just about to fix ourselves some dinner."

For an instant Chandra thought the other woman would protest the rather summary invitation to leave, but Marilyn Hastings rapidly got herself back under control and, if anything, her smile widened.

"I can take a hint, darling," she murmured gently, getting gracefully to her feet. She glided over to Reid as he uncoiled at once and stood up. Putting out the red-tipped fingernails, Marilyn lightly touched his tanned cheek and fixed her ex-husband with a very understanding look that effectively left Chandra out of the scene.

"It's all right, Reid, you don't have to pretend to me. I know I hurt you badly when I left. So badly," she added as Reid's mouth tightened grimly, "that you swore never to marry again." Marilyn turned to Chandra, who waited quietly on the hassock. "It's sweet of you to help him put up a smokescreen, Chandra, but I know the truth."

She stepped quickly for the door, turning to fling an understanding glance back at the pair in the living room. "Really, darling," she admonished Reid, her hand on the doorknob, "it's not quite fair to use her like this, is it? The poor little hired hostess might start getting notions of a genuine marriage!"

An instant later the door slammed shut behind her.

Chandra glanced uneasily at Reid, who was staring silently at the door, a set expression around his mouth, his eyes hard.

"Reid?" she ventured softly, putting her hand on his arm. "Don't worry about it. She was just being spiteful."

He shook his head, turning the gray-blue gaze on her upturned face. "I *am* worried," he confessed unexpectedly. "The woman is poison. The really disgusting part is that I knew it when I married her!"

Chandra arched an eyebrow but refrained from asking the obvious question.

"Because," he said, just as if she had asked, "she was beautiful, talented—she's an artist, you know—and I thought we had an understanding." He smiled a twisted, rueful smile. "I thought we both wanted the same things out of life here in southern California. We didn't. It was as simple and as complicated as that."

"You don't have to explain."

He cupped her face between rough palms, his gaze suddenly very intent. "Did you think I was using you when I told her you were my fiancée, Chandra?"

She smiled, eyes warm and bright. "Of course not. She has it all backward, doesn't she? You're the one protecting me, not vice-versa! Come on, I want to put my clothes in your dryer so I can get out of this robe!"

She took his hand and led him back out to the hot tub, where they collected the wet garments. Reid's mood was lightening every second now that Marilyn had gone, Chandra realized in satisfaction.

"I shall never be able to look at another hot tub again without thinking of your charming clumsiness," he remarked, fishing the scrap of torn briefs out of the pool.

"How many times do I have to explain about my poor depth perception?" Chandra complained, scooping up her ripped blouse and eyeing it ruefully. She would never be able to repair it. "Personally, it's your rather primitive seduction technique that I'll be thinking of the next time I see a hot tub. Look at my blouse! It's ruined!"

He grinned as she dangled it in front of his nose accusingly. "I'll buy you another."

"Promises, promises," she grumbled, wringing it out. "I'm lucky to have my jeans to go home in! I'll have to borrow one of your T-shirts, I suppose . . ." She broke off as she realized he was studying her with a measuring glance.

"How soon will you move in with me, Chandra?" he asked quietly.

She went still, meeting his straightforward, questioning eyes.

"As soon as you want me," she said honestly.

He nodded, satisfied. "Good. It takes three days to get a wedding license . . ."

"A license!" Chandra's hazel eyes went very wide as she stared at him in open disbelief.

"We can apply for it on Monday," he went on just as if she wasn't looking quite speechless.

"Reid, what are you saying? You don't have to get married just because you told your ex-wife that tale about being engaged!"

"Yes," he said implacably, "I do."

"That's ridiculous!"

"What's ridiculous about it?" he charged, a frown furrowing his forehead as he scanned her tense face. "You want marriage, Chandra. You've implied that from the beginning. Almost the first thing you said to me the morning after we made love was that it was wives who moved in with their husbands. Mistresses kept their own homes and their freedom."

"Reid," she began belligerently, not knowing whether to laugh or to cry, "I appreciate your motives in telling Marilyn that we were engaged, even though she didn't believe it. But I don't need that much protection. I can stand a few snide remarks. After all, a lot of people out here don't bother with wedding vows. Our relationship will be accepted quite readily by your friends . . ."

"I want our relationship accepted by everyone! Including you!" he almost snapped.

"Me!"

"Yes, you! I don't want there to be any more talk about my rights or lack of them. I don't want you to think like a mistress. Nor do I want you continually keeping an eye out for the real knight in shining armor. With my luck he's likely to show up someday after all and if you're not married you'll feel free to fall into his arms!"

"Oh, Reid," she whispered gently, eyes wondering. "Is that what you're afraid of? That I'll still be secretly searching for a fairy-tale hero?"

"I'm a realist, Chandra," he told her stonily. "I know you haven't really relinquished your childish dreams. I can't make them all come true because I'm not cut out to

150

be Sir Lancelot, as I found out this week. But I can at least offer you a ring to go with an honest relationship."

"When did you decide all this?" Chandra asked, shaken.

"I think it finally clicked when Marilyn walked into the garden and looked at you as if you were a cheap tramp." His jaw tightened.

"So you are still trying to protect me," she smiled ruefully.

He shrugged. "I suppose it's got something to do with that. All I know is that I didn't want her looking at you like that and I didn't want you thinking of yourself as still free in some sense."

"So add possessiveness to protectiveness and we have the sum of your motives, is that it?" she charged, trying to keep her voice light.

"Don't worry about my motives," he told her forcefully. "I know what I'm doing."

"Do you?"

"Yes, damnit! Now stop arguing and let's go get some dinner. Maybe I will make those margaritas. I could use one!"

"There's just one condition I'm going to make," Chandra declared, digging in her bare toes as he made to take her arm.

He swung around, prepared to demolish any more resistance. "What's that?"

"I want permission to redecorate the house."

"Redecorate!" He looked astounded.

"Your ex-wife did the present scheme, didn't she?"

"Well, yes, but I don't see . . ."

"I hate it."

"Oh." He looked a little nonplussed. "I hadn't really thought about it one way or another. It was always there!"

"Do I get my condition?"

"Hell, you can paint the whole thing purple, if you like! Of course you can redecorate!"

151

"Thank you," Chandra said politely. Lifting her head regally, she stepped past him to lead the way back to the house. Men sometimes displayed an incredible lack of understanding.

Two hours later Chandra was once again deposited politely on her own doorstep.

"I'll pick you up in the morning and take you to that restaurant so you can collect the Porsche," Reid said, bending to brush her lips in a light caress.

"Okay."

"Monday at lunch we can get the license."

"Okay."

"And then Monday night we can celebrate one of the shortest engagements on record. I'll pick up some champagne and steaks."

"Okay."

"You're awfully agreeable tonight," he observed suspiciously.

"Most women are when they're about to get married. It's after the wedding that they turn into shrews," she explained kindly, eyes dancing.

"But I've already discovered the secret for handling your temper, haven't I?" he grinned, a devil looking out of his gray-blue gaze. "A good dunking in the hot tub seems to bring you back in line very nicely."

"You're living in a fool's paradise if you think I'm going to be that easy to handle," she warned in a slow drawl.

"Probably," he agreed ruefully, "but I'll cope. Wondering why I'm back to leaving you on the doorstep with only a good-night kiss?"

"Nope. I already know the answer to that."

He lifted one brow interrogatingly. "What conclusion has your tiny little brain come to about it?"

"I figure I already wore you out for the evening with that little scene in the hot tub," she retorted smoothly.

"Wore me out!" he yelped, clearly incensed. He gave

152

her a short, crisp shake. "You're playing with fire, my girl! If it weren't for my new resolve . . ."

"What new resolve?" she asked interestedly, not feeling at all intimidated.

"Out of the goodness of my heart I've decided you deserve some sort of courtship, and since my efforts this past week were all for nothing due to your failure to understand my intent, I'm going to try to make your three-day engagement somewhat memorable." He smiled at her with unabashed expectancy.

"You look as if you expect some sort of medal," she noted, grinning.

"Wait and see," he advised, evidently pleased with himself.

The yellow roses were waiting for Chandra Monday morning at the office. She walked in the door to find Alicia popping them into water and hanging the card in an appropriate spot around one of the gorgeous flowers.

"From a grateful client?" Chandra asked, moving forward to sniff delightedly.

"In a manner of speaking," Alicia chuckled, pointing to the card. She waited as Chandra glanced at the scrawled note. She'd never seen his handwriting, but somehow she recognized it instantly.

"Reid!"

"That party must have been one heck of a success," Alicia noted cheerfully, blue eyes dancing.

Chandra flushed. "I'm going to marry him, Alicia," she confessed.

"I can't claim to be terribly surprised! Had a feeling it would come to this that first day when I saw the way he looked at you."

"You did? I didn't know until last night!" Chandra muttered, thinking her friend couldn't possibly have realized how unlikely the prospect actually was up until the previous evening.

"Well, if you don't mind my saying so, you always were a bit blind when it came to men," the older woman observed complacently.

Chandra refrained from pointing out that three marriages didn't exactly indicate any great intuitive knowledge of the opposite sex on Alicia's part, either. But she could afford to be generous now. She was in love.

She was glad of the roses sitting benignly on her desk an hour later when Marilyn Hastings walked blithely into the office. The visible evidence of Reid's intentions helped ward off some of the devastating impact of a visit from an ex-wife.

Alicia's blue eyes held cool appraisal and disapproval as she showed the other woman into Chandra's office, even though she couldn't possibly have known who Marilyn really was. But then, Marilyn Hastings was the sort of woman other women instinctively didn't like, Chandra decided spitefully as she nodded politely.

"What can I do for you, Miss Hastings?" Chandra began formally, fiercely glad the woman had elected to go back to using her own name after the divorce. Probably a step toward "finding herself." Whatever the reason, Chandra was in favor of it. She didn't care for the idea of addressing a Mrs. Devlin.

Marilyn, fashionably dressed in sleek pants and high heels, settled languidly into a chair and surveyed Chandra's equally fashionable designer shirt and jeans.

"I know you won't welcome this," Marilyn began coolly, a wry smile playing around her pretty mouth, "I certainly wouldn't have welcomed it when I was on the point of marrying Reid, but I've come to give you a little advice."

"You're quite right. I'm not in the mood for it," Chandra said stiffly.

"I knew you wouldn't be, but in a way, I kind of feel a duty to give it, regardless. I'll keep it short and simple, Chandra Madison. Reid Devlin has the morals of an alley

154

cat. He's the type of man who should never marry. And, to give him his due, he usually recognizes that fact and sticks to the casual affair. But once in a while, as he did with me, he gets carried away and decides to offer marriage."

Chandra said nothing, ignoring the implication that Reid had a string of discarded wives lying around the countryside.

"Miss Hastings, I have no wish to discuss my future husband with you . . ."

"You don't have to, my dear," Marilyn chuckled knowingly. "I'm well aware of his, shall we say, abilities. He's an extremely virile man. Who should know that better than I?"

Chandra barely concealed a wince at the reminder of the intimacy Reid had once shared with this woman.

"Unfortunately," Marilyn Hastings continued without pause, "that particular quality probably contributes toward his general inability to resist anything reasonably attractive in the female line. Why do you think I left him, Chandra?" she concluded meaningfully. "On the surface he had everything I wanted in a man. He's successful, good in bed, and he's got a certain . . . style."

"I'm sure you had your reasons," Chandra began firmly. "Look, Miss Hastings, I've got a business to run here, so if you don't mind . . ."

"I left him because I got tired of coming home to find him introducing other women to the pleasures of a hot tub! Don't you understand, Chandra? If you marry him, it's going to be you who walks into the garden some afternoon and finds some strange woman wrapped in one of your towels!"

Marilyn Hastings' attractive features shaped themselves into sober, intent warning as she leaned forward dramatically.

"My relationship with Reid appears to be on a slightly different basis from the one you had," Chandra got out

155

vengefully, getting to her feet behind the desk and facing the other woman with a grim expression.

"Any relationship Reid becomes involved in is based on only one thing, Chandra. Sex! I've told you, he's out for what he can get and he loses interest in women the way a small boy loses interest in one of his toys!"

"That's going to be my problem, isn't it?" Chandra challenged bitingly. "Will you please leave?"

"I'm only trying to warn you!"

"I don't want your warnings. Furthermore, you can't possibly be fit to give me advice of any kind! Any woman who would decorate a home the way you decorated Reid's obviously has no understanding of him at all!"

"Why, you little tramp! How dare you act as if you're something out of the ordinary just because you got a proposal out of Reid? You'll be lucky if the marriage lasts six months!"

"Last night you didn't even believe we were engaged!" Chandra shot back.

"Oh, I believe in the engagement. I've had time to think about it, you see. And I remember one thing about Reid Devlin. He doesn't bother with social lies. He probably has asked you to marry him. All I'm saying is don't get carried away with the gesture! You'll find yourself filing for divorce within months, just as I did. Unless, of course, you've got an extremely tolerant nature!"

Marilyn was on her feet and swinging toward the door before Chandra could get another word out in protest. She watched in stunned silence as the other woman walked out, and only after the outside office door slammed shut did she realize she was trembling. She sank back into the seat.

"What was that all about?" Alicia demanded, leaning calmly in the doorway, her arms folded across her chest, eyes alert.

"The ex-wife," Chandra admitted dryly. There was no

point denying it. Alicia must have heard much of the conversation.

"Well, life is not without its little thorns, is it?" Alicia noted philosophically, straightening. "Are you going to let her bother you?"

"She'd bother anybody!" Chandra growled, leaping to her feet in restless annoyance.

"True, but you know what I mean. Are you going to let her scare you off Reid?"

Chandra swiveled to look at her friend. "No," she said with sudden calm. "No, I'm not. I've made some mistakes in my judgment of men, Alicia, but this isn't one of them. I know it."

"Good. Then we can forget about that little episode, hmm?"

Chandra's mouth turned downward in self-disgust. "I'm not sure I can exactly *forget* about it, but I can ignore it!"

"That's the spirit. Life can get a bit rough out here in the fast lane, Chandra," Alicia informed her quietly. "One has to move pretty quickly to keep up."

"What's that supposed to mean?" Chandra demanded, breaking into a grin. "Some enigmatic warning?"

Alicia smiled affectionately. "I'm only saying I think Reid Devlin's worth fighting for. Don't be cowed by the competition."

"You think she wants him back?" Chandra asked, her flash of humor gone.

"Very badly. Why else would she bother with all those lies? Women like her don't feel any social obligation to warn other women of real danger. She's trying to make trouble."

Chandra nodded thoughtfully. "Still, I don't see what harm she can do. Reid was very firm with her last night when she first showed up. And I as much as told her I don't believe a word of what she was trying to imply."

"Just be careful."

"I will. I haven't got much choice."

But the perils of the day, she reflected at five minutes to twelve, weren't yet over. She knew that when she looked up at the sound of the outer door opening and saw, not Reid coming to collect her for lunch and a wedding license, but Kirby Latimer.

"Oh, my God," she muttered wretchedly. Just what she needed.

There was no point hoping Alicia would fend him off, either, as the other woman had already left for lunch.

"Hello, Chandra," Kirby said easily, walking forward to lounge in her doorway with casual familiarity. "I've come to take you to lunch."

She flicked an uninterested glance over the handsome, dark-haired, blue-eyed journalist she had once thought she loved and shook her head. "Sorry, Kirby, I've already got plans for lunch. You didn't really expect me to go out with you, anyway, did you?" she added derisively.

He straightened and walked forward, blue eyes traveling over her figure as she sat firmly behind the desk. She saw the outer attraction she had always seen in Kirby. He was wearing a black, long-sleeved shirt, black jeans and a silver chain around his neck. The outfit gave his dark handsomeness a faintly devilish look that was undeniably interesting at first glance. But today Chandra could only wonder how she'd been so blind to the very unappealing interior qualities. Had she really thought she'd found her knight when she'd run into Kirby Latimer? She must have been crazy. California crazy.

"Still angry, honey?" he murmured softly, circling her desk and perching himself easily on a corner to smile down at her with his charming, boyish grin. "I thought I'd given you enough time to cool off after Devlin's party."

"You did," she informed him flippantly. "All I feel now is disgust. I'd like you to leave, Kirby." Good heavens! Was she going to spend the whole day throwing people out of her office?

"Chandra, Chandra," he drawled, flicking her cheek with his finger, his eyes reproachful. "How can you talk like that after all we meant to each other?"

"Strangely enough, I'm not finding it a bit difficult. Please leave, Kirby!"

"Remember that little place where we used to have lunch? The one with the fantastic crab?" he coaxed as she shied away from his hand.

"You took me there only once, Kirby. Don't act as if it were our special place!" She got to her feet, reaching firmly for her purse. "I want you out of here. Now!"

"I don't believe you, honey," he murmured, sliding closer to block her exit around the desk. He started to reach for her shoulders when the sandpapery voice from the doorway cut across both of them with the force of a whiplash.

"Believe her, Latimer, or I'll put you out myself. In pieces."

"Devlin! What are you doing here?" Kirby Latimer whirled first in shock and then in annoyance as he took in the sight of the larger man filling Chandra's doorway.

"He's taking me to lunch," Chandra put in quickly, anxious to head off a major disaster. "Now, if you'll excuse me, Kirby . . ."

"Of course he will excuse you, won't you, Latimer?" Reid drawled with soft menace as she edged around Kirby and started toward Reid.

Kirby covered his startled reaction to the obvious intimacy between the other two with a cool glance of scorn aimed at Chandra.

"Don't tell me," he mocked as Reid wrapped a protective arm around her shoulders, "that the little twosome you were trying to engineer the night of the party actually took shape!" Before she could respond he swung challenging blue eyes to Reid's glacial gaze. "Don't be misled, Devlin. She's only using you to get back at me. We'd had a slight misunderstanding that night and . . ."

"And Chandra wound up in my bed," Reid finished with pure heavy-handed male satisfaction. "Which is where she's staying, Latimer, so get lost."

"Your bed!" Angry blue eyes turned on Chandra's tense face. "You spent the night with him? After leaving me dangling for damn-near a month?" He looked positively incensed, she thought gleefully. "Of all the cheap little . . ."

"One more word, Latimer, and I'll close your mouth for you," Reid said with a definite anticipation. Chandra felt the arm around her shoulder tighten in readiness.

"That's enough, Kirby," she said hurriedly. "It's time you left. You and I have nothing anymore. We never had much to begin with. Perhaps it was some instinct that kept me out of your bed. I don't like liars."

"And I suppose you think Devlin's got some monopoly on telling the truth?" Latimer growled as he made furiously for the door. "I've got news for you, you stupid broad, I've heard he's had a string of women since his divorce . . ."

"String is the operative word." She couldn't resist smiling sweetly as he glared at her from the outer door. "One at a time. He doesn't try to maintain two relationships at a time like you were going to attempt to do!"

"You probably think he's going to marry you. . . ."

"I am," Reid broke in coldly. "Three days from now. And that's really all I can allow you to say, Latimer," he added, dropping his arm from Chandra's shoulders and starting toward the younger man with clear purpose.

Kirby didn't wait to see what would happen next. He left with a loud slam of the door.

"Stifle the adrenaline, Reid, please," Chandra ordered weakly as she saw his large hand close over the doorknob. "I'd rather not have my parking lot cluttered with bodies. Bad for the image!"

There was a fractional hesitation on his part and Chandra knew he was seriously considering carrying out the action his instincts were demanding. She held her breath and then saw some of the tension leave his large frame.

"Reid," she continued softly as he turned bleak eyes to face her, "you don't think I . . . I encouraged him or anything, do you?" She couldn't bear it if he didn't trust her, Chandra realized sadly.

"No," he said with welcome assurance. "I trust you, Chandra. You couldn't look at me with those big hazel eyes and successfully lie." He stalked slowly back to where she stood waiting a little nervously.

"But, sweetheart," he went on very carefully, emphasizing each word, "if I ever walk in and find another strange man chasing you around your desk I'm going to see that you lose your business license for good! I'll chain you to the kitchen sink, instead!"

"Oh, Reid!" she mumbled, throwing herself against his chest with a broken little laugh.

"Nice flowers, huh?" he inquired, folding her close and glancing over the top of her head to where the yellow roses sat in solitary glory on her desk.

"They're beautiful. Thank you," she mumbled into his shirt.

"Wait until you see what's coming tomorrow!"

"You sound as if you're enjoying the courtship ritual. I thought you had decided displaying plumage was for the birds. Literally."

He sighed extravagantly, leading her out of the office with the air of a resigned man. "I've told you before, Chandra Madison. You make me go a little crazy."

CHAPTER TEN

When the lavishly delicate emerald and diamond ring arrived the next morning attached to an equally beautiful bouquet, the doubts Chandra had been holding under the surface finally broke free.

What in the world did she think she was doing, she asked herself wretchedly as she sat behind her desk staring at the ring, by marrying a man who didn't love her? A man who wanted her, granted. A man who wanted to give her his protection, to take care of her, but who didn't love her!

How long would his interest last? He would never make any promises he knew he couldn't keep, so she wasn't even going to hear the fantasy vows traditional at the wedding service. Reid would probably substitute his own for the civil ceremony. Perhaps they should fly to Las Vegas. After all, no one believed in Las Vegas weddings!

She chewed the unhappy thought over for a while and then pushed back her chair resolutely. It was time to feed the vicious Henderson parrot, and Chandra welcomed the diversion.

It was after she'd fed the irritable bird that she decided to do something she had never done before. She decided to play truant from the office for a couple of hours. There was a Renaissance arts and crafts fair scheduled to begin in Balboa Park, and on a whim she decided to browse.

The hot sunshine combined with the brightly colored stalls and exotic handmade ware proved a therapeutic combination. Chandra wandered from display to display, sipping at a cold lemonade and letting the noisy market atmosphere help put her problem into perspective. The warm grass smelled good in the heat of the day, and the jugglers, costumed craftspeople, and wandering minstrels made her relax.

Idly she left a stall selling delicate crystal animals and headed for one featuring pottery. She told herself she wasn't really looking for anything in particular, but when she walked past a leathercraft table something made her stop.

An intricately carved leather belt with a most unusual buckle lay shining in the sun. The kind of belt Reid might wear with his jeans, Chandra found herself thinking as she lifted the supple leather for closer inspection. The buckle was what was really drawing her attention, however, and she smiled wryly to herself as she gazed at the excellent metalwork.

It was not a gaudy thing, as were many of those lying next to it, but a neatly worked design of a mounted knight. A knight in shining armor. And it was perfect.

"Will this belt fit through the loops of a pair of jeans?" she asked the stall owner, who was dressed in a flowing Renaissance costume complete with feathered hat.

The twentieth-century bearded face behind the hat grinned at her cheerfully.

"Lady, I wouldn't dream of making belts that didn't fit jeans. I'd be out of business!"

With a laugh, Chandra paid for her purchase and saw it slipped into a bag. She hoped it fit Reid's lean waist. More than that, she added dryly, she hoped he'd like it enough to wear it!

Something in her was satisfied at finding the belt. Without any further qualms, Chandra headed for the Porsche.

Only to find, to her horror, that some fool in a brand-new Mercedes and another one in an elegant Jaguar had wedged her car tightly into its slot. Chandra took one look at the tiny maneuvering space left for her in which to extract the Porsche and knew she didn't dare risk it. The thought of facing angry owners of either of the other cars was too much and she just didn't trust her own ability to get the Porsche safely out of the tight space.

With a groan, she climbed the grassy knoll to the entrance of one of the park's museums and found a telephone.

"Chandra?" Alicia sounded concerned. "Where are you?"

"Trapped in a parking lot," Chandra muttered dramatically. Rapidly she explained the situation. "I'll just have to wait until one or the other of the cars is moved. It shouldn't be too long. Any messages?"

"Nothing you'd want to respond to," Alicia replied blandly.

"Meaning?"

"Meaning that Marilyn Hastings called."

"Oh, Lord! What did she want?"

"Beats me. I told her you were unavailable for the day."

"Thanks," Chandra breathed.

"Hang on, there's someone on the other line."

Chandra's phone went silent as Alicia answered the new call. A couple of seconds later the older woman was back on the line.

"Chandra, it's Reid. He wants to know where you are!" Alicia sounded anxious. "Shall I tell him about your, uh, predicament?"

"Don't you dare! He'd laugh himself hoarse! Just give him some line about me going shopping. I don't care what you say but don't try and explain this. The man has no understanding of depth-perception problems!"

Alicia chuckled and left the line again. A moment later she was back. "It's okay. I told him you were out shopping and would give him a call when you got back."

"Thanks, Alicia. I won't forget this."

"Uh-huh. See that you remember it the next time we have to feed a parrot!"

164

For the next hour Chandra wandered in and out of the Aerospace Museum. She had just finished looking at the astronaut display when she took a quick glance outside and noticed the Mercedes driver had removed his car. Hastily she removed hers and headed for the office. It was getting late. Alicia would be getting ready to go home for the day.

When she reached the office Alicia was gone but the message to meet Reid at his office was on her desk. With a small frown Chandra read it through quickly. Something about him being tied up in a meeting and could she come by after work. They'd go out to dinner nearby.

Chandra had never been to the office of the construction firm Reid owned, but she had the address and with only a little difficulty found it near La Jolla.

The corporation was housed in a modern building designed, she saw, with solar heating panels and a distant view of the ocean. She wondered if the solar-heating arrangements were an experiment on Reid's part. Many construction firms in southern California were offering such designs now.

The black Ferrari was in the parking lot along with a scattering of other cars. Most of the people who worked in the building appeared to have left for the day.

Following the discreet signs Chandra made her way down a carpeted hall to a suite of offices labeled "President." The outer office was darkened, she noticed, as she pushed open the door. Reid's secretary must have left by now. But there was a light on behind the inner door, and as Chandra started forward, her footsteps clicking lightly on the parquet flooring, she heard a woman's voice. Marilyn Hastings' voice.

"Reid, you've got to tell her! You know you don't love her! Do you think it's fair to marry her under the circumstances? You'll break her heart and you know you'll only be doing it to hurt me!"

165

The voice, Chandra decided wryly, was absolutely heartrending.

"Marilyn." Reid's voice came back with cool annoyance. "My secretary has returned. Would you mind keeping your voice down?"

Chandra lifted her hand to knock on Reid's door just as Marilyn said, "She deserves to know, Reid. She deserves to know that nothing is over between us. That we've been seeing each other since the divorce."

"Are you threatening to tell her that?" Reid asked in a very deadly voice.

Chandra shivered and knocked once. Then, without giving anyone inside a chance to respond, she pushed open the door.

To find Marilyn nestled in Reid's arms.

Several things happened almost simultaneously. Chandra met Reid's eyes over the top of Marilyn's lovely red head and saw the brilliant, totally unexpected flash of pain in the glacial pools.

Marilyn lifted herself away from Reid's chest in startled, rueful dismay, turning to look at Chandra with a patently false expression of apologetic understanding.

And Chandra looked at both of them and couldn't help it. She smiled. A wide, amused smile that warmed her eyes and threatened to escalate into outright laughter.

"Chandra!" Marilyn exclaimed swiftly, moving guiltily away from Reid, who was simply staring at his fiancée as if he'd never seen her before. "I'm so sorry you had to find out like this. It was nothing, really. Just a little farewell kiss from an ex-wife. Isn't that right, darling?" she added, glancing pleadingly at Reid for confirmation.

He ignored her. He was still staring at Chandra, whose smile had broadened slightly.

"What are you doing here?" he ground out heavily, sounding dazed.

"I got your message," Chandra began, and saw the blank expression in his brilliant eyes. "Oh, I see," she added quickly, sliding a humorous sidelong look at Marilyn. "That was part of the setup."

"Setup!" the other woman exploded. "What are you talking about?"

"Why, the little scene you just choreographed for my benefit, of course," she explained kindly.

"Is that what you think this was?" Marilyn demanded with a smoothness in her sultry voice that told Chandra she had recovered from the unexpected mockery in her intended victim's eyes. "Well, I suppose that's as good an explanation as any," she went on easily. "Just keep telling yourself that, Chandra dear, on the evenings when Reid works late at the office and on those days when he's called out of town on business."

"Please go away, Marilyn," Chandra said politely, meeting the other woman's venemous look with a placid expression. "You're just not important around here."

"Why, you little . . ."

"Do as she says, Marilyn," Reid interrupted coldly. "Go away. She's quite right. You're not important to either Chandra or myself."

"Is that so?" Marilyn hissed, her spiteful eyes on Chandra's calm face. "Will you still be thinking that when you move into the house I decorated? When you use my towels? My furniture? Look at my paintings?"

"Haven't you heard?" Chandra smiled gently. "I'm going to paint the whole place purple."

"Purple!" Marilyn shrieked, confirming Chandra's initial impression that the woman had no sense of humor.

"You didn't think I'd let Reid continue to live in that cold-bloodedly decorated house, did you? Good-bye, Marilyn."

"Purple!" Marilyn whirled to confront Reid, who eyed her expressionlessly. "You're going to let her do that?"

"Chandra can do whatever she wants," he said softly, his mind clearly on something else entirely. "As long as she marries me."

"You've got a lot of nerve calling me cold-blooded," Marilyn snapped as she picked up her purse and headed toward where Chandra stood at the door. "You're the one marrying a man who doesn't know the meaning of love. But maybe it's a case of like attracting like? Why *are* you marrying him, Chandra? Because he's good in bed? Because he's successful? Don't try telling him you love him. Not now, not after the way you laughed when you walked in and found him with another woman!"

"I didn't walk in and find him making love to you, though, Marilyn," Chandra said very carefully, facing Reid's ex-wife quite honestly. "I walked in and found you'd set him up. You'd lured me here precisely so I'd find you in his arms, didn't you?"

"And it didn't seem to bother you one bit!" Marilyn countered triumphantly.

"Well, you are turning out to be somewhat annoying," Chandra conceded.

"Annoying!"

"But not very important, as Reid and I have just told you. Why stick around to hear more?"

"Have it your way, Chandra Madison," the redhead muttered. "But don't say I didn't warn you about him. The morals of an alley cat. I'm beginning to think you both deserve each other!"

An instant later the door slammed behind her. Chandra gazed after the departed woman and had a hunch Marilyn Hastings wouldn't be back. She'd tried her biggest guns and the ambush had failed. The woman was a survivor. She'd go on to other things. Other men.

With a soft smile Chandra turned back to meet Reid's eyes. He still had that faintly dazed look but there was a new determination in him. Something she couldn't put a name to looked out at her from the deep ice.

"Chandra," he said, the sandpaper raw and rasping in his voice. "I have to talk to you."

"It's all right, Reid," she soothed. "I understand her. I know she planned this whole thing. . . ."

"No, that's not what I mean," he muttered, waving aside her placating words with a dismissing sweep of his hand. He stood very tall and very formidable beside the mahogany desk, the copper in his hair catching the last gleaming rays of the evening sun.

And for the first time since she had walked in the office door, Chandra stopped smiling with her eyes. The scene with Marilyn had been irritating, but, ultimately, not critical. Now, however, something very critical, indeed, had entered the atmosphere. She could feel it emanating from him, and real fear touched her spine.

"No, Reid," she whispered a little thickly, "don't say it. I don't want you to say it."

"Chandra . . ." he began, the pain leaping back to life in his eyes.

"Reid, forget it, please!" she begged, moving forward to stand in front of him, gazing desperately up into his face. "It's too late."

"The hell it is!" he growled, reaching for her arms with both hands.

"It is! It is!" she cried hysterically, swept over the edge of her normal reasoning process by the new and terrible fear he had invoked. "I won't let you back out of it! You're going to marry me! You promised! I already bought you a wedding present!" she concluded miserably.

"Back out of it! What are you talking about?" He gave her a brief shake that brought the knot of tawny hair cascading down around her ears.

She returned his exasperated glare with a pitiful expression. "You're going to tell me you can't marry me because your honesty won't let you take advantage of my love, aren't you? You're going to say that you don't love me and that you can't bring yourself to destroy any more of my illusions! But, Reid, it's all right! I promise you! I'm willing to take what you can offer. It's so much more than I had any right to expect . . ."

"Chandra, you little idiot," he groaned, hauling her close against his chest. "Stop putting words in my mouth!"

Crushed against his shirt, Chandra drew a shaky breath and closed her eyes in unbearable hope.

"I'm trying to say that I love you, Chandra," Reid whispered heavily, his lips in her hair as he clamped her to his hard frame. "My God! How I love you!"

"Love me! Reid! Do you really?" Chandra stood perfectly still as she waited for him to confirm a future for which she hadn't even dared to hope.

"Since the first day I saw you, I think," he purred in wonder. "But fool that I am, I didn't have enough sense to recognize it until . . ."

"Until when?" she breathed, aware of an incredible happiness and an enormous relief.

"Until you walked in that door and saw Marilyn in my arms," he admitted with total honesty.

"Just now?" she squeaked, pulling slightly away from him to stare up into his drawn, tense face. She saw the hungry flames leaping below the surface of the ice in his eyes and waited. "What in the world was so revealing about what happened a few minutes ago?"

"It wasn't anything you or Marilyn did," he muttered thickly. "It was the horror I felt when I looked up and saw you standing in the doorway."

"But I don't understand . . ." she began, perplexed. She had been smiling when she stood in the doorway, mildly amused by Marilyn's stupid ploy.

"I saw you and the first thing that hit me was the impossibility of trying to explain my ex-wife in my arms. It took me a minute to realize you weren't buying her little setup and during that minute I thought that if you were so hurt by it that you walked out on me I would truly go crazy. Not just California crazy, but insane! Chandra, I

170

was literally terrified for a moment and suddenly I realized why."

"Reid . . ."

"I love you, Chandra," he said again slowly, the note of wonder still in his voice and now in his eyes. "I love you so much that I was on the verge of panic at the thought of losing you. I'd never felt that way about any woman and once I recognized that I recognized a lot of other things as well."

"Such as?" Chandra invited, utterly entranced. She looked up at him with shining eyes but there was a certain seriousness in his gaze that told her he was still working things out in his mind. Well, she wouldn't press him, she would let him tell her in his own words and in his own time.

"Such as the fact that I'd been so eager to explain my need of you by saying that it was only desire and a wish to protect you," he began slowly.

And Chandra spoiled her good intentions by interrupting cheekily. "You mean you don't really desire me?"

"I shouldn't dignify that with an answer," he scolded, a gleam appearing in the intent eyes with which he raked her face.

"Humor me," she encouraged laughingly, her hands on his shoulders, enjoying the feel of his muscles as they shifted slightly under her fingertips. She was enjoying everything about him, she realized dimly. The scent of his warm body, the hardness of his thighs, the sandpaper and velvet of his voice. It seemed to her in that moment she would never be able to get enough of this man.

"Humor you?" he repeated with an obliging, crooked little smile. "Are you going to try and pretend that you really don't know how I lie alone in bed and ask myself whether or not I'll be able to survive until morning without you? Are you going to tell me you don't understand how much I love the feel of your body next to mine? Don't you know that when I touch your soft breasts and feel them come alive under my hand that I enter another world? Haven't I told you that the inside of your thighs feel like silk? That your mouth is a cave of warmth and honey? That possessing you is the only thing on earth for which I'd sacrifice anything I own?"

"Oh!"

Chandra felt the heat suffuse her face as the intimate words fell around her like flowers and the devouring gaze lapped at her like the sea.

"So much for desire," she gasped weakly, clinging to his shoulders to steady herself.

"Now I suppose you want to hear that I haven't lost my wish to protect you," he murmured, aware of her helplessness and clearly enjoying the effect he was having on her senses.

Chandra couldn't answer that one, but she listened breathlessly as he issued yet another declaration of his love.

"I should have known when I couldn't bear the thought of you not living with me that my sense of protectiveness was working overtime," he whispered deeply. "No, I should have known much earlier than that," he corrected after a second's pause. "That night when I took you home and you received the call from Sherwood I felt like a crusader who's finally been handed a cause he would cheerfully kill for! I couldn't believe that I was going to have my chance with you handed to me on a silver platter but I grabbed it before you could back out of it. Somehow I had to tie you to my side, make you give me the right to protect you. I probably wasn't thinking very clearly that night. I know damn well I *was* thinking very primitively!"

"I do remember making a few weak efforts to remind you that I hadn't really accepted your 'protection,'" Chandra said a little wryly. "As I recall, you overrode my arguments!"

"I was desperate. I knew you were beginning to see me

172

as some sort of gallant defender and I was torn between wanting you to admire me and just plain wanting you! It wasn't much of a contest," he confessed wryly. "The need to try and chain you to me with the only bond I had was far too great. I wanted to have the right to take care of you for as long as you lived. The right to protect you from all the other men in the world who only wanted to use you. But a man can't just assume that sort of privilege, it has to be given to him. I was sure that if I could establish a strong enough physical bond between us, you would fully accept my protection."

"As you said," she teased lovingly, "you were thinking rather primitively!"

"Umm," he agreed ruefully. "Then the next morning when you started talking about keeping your own home and refusing to move in with me, I realized I'd pushed you too far. I'd made you accept our arrangement but I was a long way from getting out of it what I wanted. That's why I tried to behave like the gallant knight for the next few days. I wanted you to admire me as a heroic type who would perform his lady's services without making too many demands. Then you went off to that Friday night drink with the gang and I reached the end of my tether!"

"Poor Reid," she soothed sweetly, eyes dancing. "But I was getting a little desperate myself! I wasn't sure what was going on and I guess some primitive instinct was at work in my mind, too. I was trying to force your hand, I think. But it won't happen again!" she vowed suddenly.

"Learned your lesson, hmm?" he demanded, beginning to grin wickedly.

"Let's just say that it was something of a shock when you did show up, even if my subconscious had been waiting for you!" she admitted dryly.

He sobered and his expression became more searching. "Chandra, did you mean what you implied a few minutes ago when you said not to worry about taking advantage of your love? Do you love me, sweetheart?"

"Why else would I tell your ex-wife I was going to paint the house purple? Only a woman madly in love and willing to do anything to crush her rival would threaten a thing like that!"

CHAPTER ELEVEN

Chandra stood barefoot on the sandy Maui beach and watched her husband emerge from the surf, snorkel and flippers grasped in one hand. She smiled as he spotted her waiting and he came toward her with that curiously satisfied look that had been in his eyes since they'd taken their wedding vows the day before in San Diego. Very traditional vows they had been, too, Chandra reflected happily. The "until death us do part" variety.

"You were right about honeymoons," Reid said, grinning as he reached her side and took the towel she was holding for him. "They're much better suited for husbands and wives. There's more of a sense of beginning about the whole thing!"

"What brought that up?" she chuckled, flopping down beside him as he settled back on the sand. "Decide you don't miss having a mistress after all?"

"I've decided I like having both!" he murmured, leaning over to feather a kiss against her bare shoulder. "All wrapped up in one package!"

The emerald green one-piece swimsuit Chandra was wearing left considerably more than her shoulders bare but not nearly as much of her as the brief bikini she had originally chosen that morning in the Hawaiian shop. Reid, however, had squelched the intended purchase with an outraged exclamation that had taken both the saleslady and Chandra by surprise.

Stalking to the rack of suits, he'd yanked out the green

one and ordered it to be tried on without further delay. Chandra, hiding a smile, had obediently disappeared back into the changing room to reappear a few moments later in the more modest suit. Reid had nodded, apparently satisfied. Later she'd chided him for losing his southern California attitude about such things but he'd only laughed and told her she was a wife now. Which meant, Chandra was left to assume, that she was to surrender to her husband on such issues.

"Greedy man," she murmured in response to his comment about having both a wife and a mistress. She drank in the sight of his sea-wet body sprawled lazily beside her. From beneath half-lowered lashes she watched the water run off his arms in small, intricate patterns.

"Why shouldn't I be greedy? We get what we want in this life if we go after it with enough enthusiasm," he chuckled carelessly, opening his eyes to meet hers across the small stretch of sand separating them.

"You didn't exactly get what you wanted that night of the party," she retorted, determined to find a way to provoke him. He looked far too much like a large, satisfied panther. A copper-streaked panther. Her eyes closed drowsily.

"No?"

The single, drawled word brought Chandra to a sitting position in a sudden, jolting movement.

"What's that supposed to mean?" she charged, remembering anew the satisfaction she'd seen in his eyes the morning after the party. A satisfaction she'd never fully comprehended after he'd told her they hadn't made love that night.

He smiled up at her outraged expression, his eyes leaping with little ice devils. "I merely wondered what made you think I didn't get what I wanted the night of the party."

"You told me we didn't . . . I mean that I hadn't . . . hadn't done anything!" she reminded him righteously.

176

"The next morning in the shower you said . . . Reid Devlin, why *were* you looking so damned pleased with yourself that morning, anyway?"

"Because I was pleased with myself."

"Why?" she demanded starkly, ready to wreak vengeance of some sort. Perhaps she'd bury him in the sand.

"Isn't it obvious? I had you in my bed," he chuckled obligingly. "I thought everything else would fall neatly into line. How was I to know you were going to run me ragged before it was all over?"

"That's the real reason?" she demanded suspiciously.

"Would I lie to you?" he asked innocently.

Chandra collapsed onto his still-damp chest, giggling. "No, Reid, you would never, ever lie to me. If you tell me that's the way it was, I'll believe you. I think I'd believe anything you said."

"Looking at me through the eyes of love?" he teased gently, his hand moving through the wet tangle of her hair.

"Partly," she agreed complacently.

"What other reason do you have for believing me?"

"Come back to the room with me and I'll show you."

"How can I resist an invitation like that?"

Hand in hand they tramped through the sand toward the exotic hotel where they were booked for the next two weeks. It was a beautiful place on a beautiful island, and as far as Chandra was concerned it was perfect. But, then, anywhere would have been perfect.

"Imagine flying a couple of thousand miles just to look at the same ocean," Reid observed good-naturedly as they walked into the luxurious room with its lanai facing the sparkling Pacific.

"It looks different from here than it does from our home in La Jolla," Chandra insisted, heading for the bathroom to drop the sandy towels in the hamper.

"I'm glad you can tell the difference," he called after her. "Frankly, it wouldn't have mattered to me where we

177

went as long as I knew you weren't going home in the morning! Now, what about that other reason you promised to explain to me!"

Chandra poked her head around the bathroom door. "Don't you want to rinse off the sand first?"

"When have I ever refused to climb into a shower with you?" He started forward with a warning leer.

After fifteen minutes of wet struggle to keep things on an even keel, Chandra finally turned off the water and stepped out of the tub, grabbing a towel.

"Okay, okay, I'll show you the other reason!" she laughed, slipping out of the bathroom and rushing to where her suitcase stood on the bench.

She heard him following her as she bent over and located the small sack holding the belt she'd bought at the Renaissance Fair.

"About this reason," he began in anticipation, his large hands reaching out to encircle her towel-wrapped waist.

She turned in the embrace and held up the belt, a faintly tremulous smile on her lips. She loved this man and he loved her, but it suddenly occurred to Chandra that Reid Devlin might not thank her for persisting in her foolish insistence on finding a knight in shining armor.

The laughter went out of his eyes as he took the belt from her hand.

"My wedding present?" he asked quietly, examining the buckle with a probing touch.

"Yes," she whispered, waiting in an agony of suspense.

He continued to stare at the wrought metal for a moment longer and then he lifted questioning blue-gray eyes.

"Chandra, my little love, is this the other reason you'd believe anything I said? You see me as your knight in shining armor?"

"I can't help it, Reid," she said softly, standing very still as she awaited his reaction. "I've trusted you from the first. An honest man in a world full of dishonest men. It grew out of that, I think. Your protection and the knowledge that I could trust you made what other men were offering look worthless. I love you, but there's more to it than that, and I don't know how else to explain it except to say that I believe in you, too. You're the man I've spent a lifetime hoping to find. Is it any wonder I see you as my knight?"

"I guess not," he agreed with a slow smile. "Especially when you consider the fact that I see you as the lady to whom I've dedicated my life."

"Oh, Reid, I do love you!" she cried, flinging herself into his arms with complete abandon.

"And I love you, my sweet Chandra," he grated thickly in her ear as he lifted the damp hair off the back of her neck and kissed the nape. "More than words can say. Which is why, I imagine, I've spent so much time trying to get you permanently into my bed!"

He set the coiled belt carefully down onto the dresser and lifted his wife into his arms. When he set her down on the bed a moment later she lay looking up at him with all her love in her eyes. For a moment longer he simply stared down at her, absorbing the picture she made lying across the coverlet.

Then he slowly reached down and loosened the towel from where it had been anchored above her breast, unwrapping her with lazy pleasure. When she was nude, he let the towel he was wearing slip from his own waist and came down heavily beside her.

"Chandra, my darling Chandra," he rasped, pulling her into his arms.

She went willingly, her fingers stroking through the thickness of his hair and searching out the much finer hairs on his back and broad shoulders.

"Oh, Reid," she whispered brokenly as his palms swept hungrily down her body, gliding over her breasts and the curve of her stomach and back again.

The loving words flowed back and forth between them even as the loving touches did. Chandra felt her body flower beneath Reid's caresses and wondered dizzily if she'd ever grow accustomed to the pleasure of it.

He dropped a series of small kisses along her arm to the vulnerable point of her wrist and then moved to take her lips. Slowly, lingeringly, his mouth feasted on hers, drawing forth the elemental feminine surrender it sought even as her hands were at work seeking the evidence of his desire.

She heard his husky groan when she instinctively clenched her fingers into the muscular buttocks, felt the instant response of his body and exulted in it.

"You do drive me crazy, woman!"

"California crazy?" she taunted lovingly.

"No, just the old fashioned craziness a man feels for the woman he loves!"

She buried her fingers in the curling hair of his chest, teasing the male nipples with gentle kisses and letting her hair brush the tightened skin of his stomach.

Her leg somehow became entwined with his and a moment later he was using the leverage to push her back onto the bed. She felt his body covering hers, gently forcing apart her legs and moving to take the heart of her warmth with power and passion.

He claimed her as he had before, letting her body know that it could respond only to him, renewing the eternal conquest even while succumbing to the eternal feminine snare.

With love and passion she gathered him in, accepting the strength and need of his body as her mind accepted the protectiveness and possession of his instincts. They were all part of the man who was Reid Devlin. It was all a part of the way he loved.

She had been right, Chandra thought distantly as he enthralled her body, a man like this was capable of love, great love on a thousand different levels from the physical to the spiritual. Her intuition had been correct.

She rode the raging river with him once again, clinging

to his smoothly muscled back as he held her in the deepest embrace. With the mounting fury of the lovemaking she was unaware of it when her neat white teeth sank into the skin of his shoulder.

"Oh!" she moaned when he returned the caress, letting her feel the sharpness of his own teeth and then the soothing touch of his lips.

Somehow the small pain that was not a pain drove her over the limits and she was transformed into a writhing, twisting creature who delighted the man above her.

"My own little wildcat!" Reid growled, letting the small storm erupt beneath him but containing it within the boundaries of his grasp.

The passionate mockery seemed to turn her a little crazy, too, as Chandra responded by throwing all her strength into dominating the never-ending confrontation of man and woman.

Whether taken by surprise at the sudden urgency in her movements or because he was simply reveling in her response, Reid rolled onto his back, and Chandra flung herself into the role of master with a fierce passion.

She rained kisses across his chest and buried her lips in his neck. She nibbled erotically on his ears and used her hands to control the surging of his body against hers.

"Chandra!" Her name was a plea and a warning that she refused to heed. •

"Do you think you can get away with this?" he growled hoarsely as her eyes clashed momentarily with his. "You can only drive a man so far, little one!"

"How far?" she challenged, running fingertips of lightning down his waist and beyond.

"Congratulations, wife," he rasped huskily. "You just reached the limit!"

He pulled her completely down on top of him, forcing her to the rhythm of his guiding hands as he had that day in the hot tub. His muscular ankles trapped hers and she was held firmly in his power even though she had thought herself so much in command.

There was a shatteringly incoherent moment of tension and then a delicious quiet settled on the tousled bed.

Pleased with herself and with the world, Chandra lay curled against the strong body next to her, idly tracing designs on Reid's ribcage as she waited for him to open his eyes.

"Think you're going to be happy being a wife?" he eventually murmured interestedly without lifting his lashes.

"A southern Californian can handle anything."

"Southern California macho?"

"Umm."

"I've been thinking about that," he said after a moment. "Macho?"

"Southern California."

"What about it?" she inquired easily.

"I'm not sure that either one of us is quite cut out for the fast lane."

She lifted her head at that, surprised by the comment. "What makes you say that?"

He shrugged slightly, opening his eyes to meet hers at last. There was a new seriousness in the ice-colored depths. "Something tells me both of us have been looking for something else for a long time. We've found it. What do we need with southern California any longer?"

"You told me once I wouldn't be happy in a small town," she reminded him, feeling curious.

"I said that because I didn't want you getting any notions of running off and leaving San Diego before I'd had a chance to stake my claim!" he grinned.

"Is that so?" she began with mock indignation.

"I'm serious, Chandra," he said softly. "What do you think?"

"About leaving California?"

"Yes."

"We've both got businesses there," she pointed out practically.

"Between selling two successful businesses and two highly inflated homes, we'll have a nice nest egg!"

Chandra smiled. "Reid, I'd go anywhere you wished, you know that. And maybe you're right. Maybe we're not cut out for the fast lane. It was fun for a while but the truth is that until I woke up that morning in your bed, I didn't think I'd ever quite get into it!"

"Lucky I was there when you made the final transition, huh?"

"Don't show your ego like that. It's not modest."

"Sorry. Well?"

"Where did you have in mind to immigrate?" she grinned.

"The Southwest, maybe. New Mexico?"

She pretended to consider that. "Do they have hot tubs in New Mexico?"

"We could import them and sell to the locals," he offered conspiratorially. "Probably make a killing!"

"How about Porsche and Ferrari mechanics? Do they have those outside California? We drive hothouse cars, don't forget. They need proper attention."

"I'm not sure what people drive outside California but I do know there would be lots more room to park the Porsche!"

"I resent that." She thought a moment. "New Mexico sounds fine."

"I have a confession to make," Reid added as an aside. "At the wedding Alicia told me where you'd been that afternoon before you showed up on my office doorstep and extracted that declaration of love from me."

"She told you I was trapped in a parking lot?" Chandra grimaced.

"Just think, if you'd had the sense to call me to the rescue, Marilyn would never have been able to stage her little scene."

"I wouldn't have dreamed of humiliating myself to that extent!" Chandra vowed.

"Well, anyway, you have to admit that parking room is a definite consideration."

"I'll get even for that one of these days."

"My pleasure," he agreed amiably. "Speaking of that magic afternoon, did I ever get around to telling you how much it meant to have you believe me innocent of all charges?" There was a teasing note in his deep voice, but the warmth in his eyes felt like the sun and she smiled beneath its rays.

"You're an honest man," Chandra said simply. "You wouldn't be trying to seduce me and carry on an affair with another woman at the same time."

"Alicia mentioned that Marilyn had paid you a little visit, also," he said quietly.

"Alicia seems to have done quite a bit of talking after the wedding," Chandra complained. "Where was I during this lengthy conversation you two were having?"

"Drinking margaritas from my blender."

"Flying makes me nervous," she explained airily, thinking back to the small group of people who had gathered at Reid's after the ceremony.

"Did Marilyn, uh, say anything besides the obvious?" Reid persisted carefully.

"Nothing important. She doesn't know you very well."

"No," he said gently. "She doesn't. I think you are the only person on earth who knows me well. But the reason I asked is that she came down to San Diego out of more than just female curiosity."

Chandra blinked, surprised. "I know she wanted you back . . ."

He shook his head. "She wanted money. She knew the minute she saw us together that I was deadly serious about you. I think she realized I was in love before I did. So she threatened to tell you she and I were having an affair, knowing that would be the biggest rock she could hold over my head. The settlement at the time of the divorce, apparently, hasn't lasted very long. She wanted to 'renegotiate' it."

"You weren't tempted to do that, were you?" Chandra asked, appalled at the other woman's audacity.

"No, but that's the reason behind the scene in my office."

"Oh." Chandra paused. "Do you feel . . ."

"Guilty? Absolutely not. She walked out on me, remember. Besides, Marilyn has money of her own. She was just trying to pad things a bit."

"Then we can forget her." Chandra smiled again.

"Definitely. Anyhow, I'm glad you believed me after the office scene," he concluded in satisfied pleasure.

"You believed me when I explained about that fiasco in the singles bar and about Kirby being in my office," she reminded him. "You didn't like it very much, as I recall," she emphasized with a grin, "especially my going out for a drink with my friends, but you believed me when I said I had no intention of going off with anyone there."

"I suppose that was another point at which I should have realized I was hopelessly in love," he sighed ruefully. "When I found myself letting you off the hook so easily . . ."

"Easily! You pushed me into a hot tub!"

"You fell in due to natural clumsiness," he contradicted virtuously.

"Poor depth perception!"

"Whatever you say, honey. Fortunately neither your depth perception nor your clumsiness matters very much where it counts."

"Where's that?" she demanded suspiciously.

"In bed," he chuckled.

"Beast."

"A tame beast," he murmured in thickest velvet, stroking the smooth skin of her back as she lay against him. "Sworn to love and protect my lady. For always."

Chandra felt the tremor of power and love that went through him as he made his vow once again, and then she snuggled deeper into the shelter of a man's protection.

LOOK FOR NEXT MONTH'S
CANDLELIGHT ECSTASY ROMANCES™:

"THE MOST ROMANTIC NOVEL SINCE LOVE STORY."
—Good Housekeeping

Change of Heart

SALLY MANDEL

Once in a long while, a story is so bursting with charm and tenderness that its charm is irresistible.

That story is Sharlie and Brian's story, *Change of Heart*—a love story for a lifetime.

A Dell Book $2.95 (11355-5)

At your local bookstore or use this handy coupon for ordering:

Dell	**DELL BOOKS** **P.O. BOX 1000, PINEBROOK, N.J. 07058**	CHANGE OF HEART $2.95 (11355-5)

Please send me the above title. I am enclosing $ _____
(please add 75¢ per copy to cover postage and handling). Send check or money order—no cash or C.O.D.'s. Please allow up to 8 weeks for shipment.

Mr/Mrs/Miss _____

Address _____

City _____ State/Zip _____

Breathtaking sagas
of adventure
and
romance

VALERIE
VAYLE